# NADINE GORDIMER

# CRIMES OF
# CONSCIENCE

## HEINEMANN

Heinemann International Literature and Textbooks
a division of Heinemann Educational Books Ltd
Halley Court, Jordan Hill, Oxford OX2 8EJ

Heinemann Educational Books Inc.
361 Hanover Street, Portsmouth, New Hampshire, 03801, USA

Heinemann Educational Books (Nigeria) Ltd
PMB 5205, Ibadan
Heinemann Kenya Ltd
PO Box 45314, Nairobi, Kenya
Heinemann Educational Boleswa
PO Box 10103, Village Post Office, Gaborone, Botswana

LONDON   EDINBURGH   MADRID
PARIS   ATHENS   BOLOGNA   MELBOURNE
SYDNEY   AUCKLAND   SINGAPORE
TOKYO   HARARE

Series Editor: Adewale Maja-Pearce

British Library Cataloguing in Publication Data

Gordimer, Nadine 1923–
Crimes of conscience – (African writers series).
I. Title II. Series
823[F]

ISBN 0–435–90668–2

Photoset by Wilmaset, Birkenhead, Wirral
Printed and bound in Great Britain by
Cox & Wyman Ltd, Reading, Berkshire

91   92   93   94   10   9   8   7   6   5   4   3

# CONTENTS

Acknowledgements

# ACKNOWLEDGEMENTS

The publishers would like to thank the following for their permission to use copyright material:

Felix Licensing BV, for copyright in the short story, 'The Ultimate Safari' © Felix Licensing BV 1989;

Jonathan Cape, London, for 'Town and Country Lovers', 'A Soldier's Embrace', 'A Hunting Accident', 'The Termitary', and 'Oral History' from *A Soldier's Embrace* (Jonathan Cape 1980) © Nadine Gordimer 1980;

Jonathan Cape, London, and Viking Penguin Inc, New York, for 'A City of the Dead, A City of the Living', 'Blinder', 'A Correspondence Course', 'Crimes of Conscience', 'At the Rendezvous of Victory', from *Something Out There* (Jonathan Cape 1984, Viking Penguin Inc 1984, Penguin Books 1985) © Nadine Gordimer 1984.

The publishers have made every effort to trace copyright holders. We shall be very glad to hear from anyone who has been inadvertently overlooked or incorrectly cited and make the necessary changes at the first opportunity.

# 'A City of the Dead, A City of the Living'

*You only count the days if you are waiting to have a baby or you are in prison. I've had my child but I'm counting the days since he's been in this house.*

The street delves down between two rows of houses like the abandoned bed of a river that has changed course. The shebeen-keeper who lives opposite has a car that sways and churns its way to her fancy wrought-iron gate. Everyone else, including shebeen customers, walks over the stones, sand and gullies, home from the bus station. It's too far to bicycle to work in town.

The house provides the sub-economic township planner's usual two rooms and kitchen with a little yard at the back, into which his maquette figures of the ideal family unit of four fitted neatly. Like most houses in the street, it has been arranged inside and out to hold the number of people the ingenuity of necessity provides for. The garage is the home of sub-tenants. (The shebeen-keeper, who knows everything about everybody, might remember how the house came to have a garage – perhaps a taxi owner once lived there.) The front door of the house itself opens into a room that has been subdivided by greenish brocade curtains whose colour had faded and embossed pattern worn off before they were discarded in another kind of house. On one side of the curtains is a living room with just space enough to crate a plastic-covered sofa and two chairs, a coffee table with crocheted cover, vase of dyed feather flowers and oil lamp, and a radio-and-cassette-player combination with home-built speakers. There is a large varnished print of a horse with wild orange mane and flaring nostrils on the wall. The floor is cement, shined with black polish. On the other side of the curtains is a bed, a burglar-proofed window, a small table with

1

candle, bottle of anti-acid tablets and alarm clock. During the day a frilly nylon nightgown is laid out on the blankets. A woman's clothes are in a box under the bed. In the dry cleaner's plastic sheath, a man's suit hangs from a nail.

A door, never closed, leads from the living room to the kitchen. There is a sink, which is also the bathroom of the house, a coal-burning stove finned with chrome like a 1940s car, a pearly-blue formica dresser with glass doors that don't slide easily, a table and plastic chairs. The smell of cooking never varies: mealie-meal burning, curry overpowering the sweet reek of offal, sour porridge, onions. A small refrigerator, not connected, is used to store margarine, condensed milk, tinned pilchards; there is no electricity.

Another door, with a pebbled glass pane in its upper half, is always kept closed. It opens off the kitchen. Net curtains reinforce the privacy of the pebbled glass: the privacy of the tenant of the house, Samson Moreke, whose room is behind there, shared with his wife and baby and whichever of their older children spends time away from other relatives who take care of them in country villages. When all the children are in their parents' home at once, the sofa is a bed for two; others sleep on the floor in the kitchen. Sometimes the sofa is not available, since adult relatives who find jobs in the city need somewhere to live. Number 1907 Block C holds – has held – eleven people; how many it could hold is a matter of who else has nowhere to go. This reckoning includes the woman lodger and her respectable succession of lovers behind the green brocade curtain, but not the family lodging in the garage.

In the backyard, Samson Moreke, in whose name tenancy of Number 1907 Block C is registered by the authorities, has put up poles and chicken wire and planted Catawba grapevines that make a pleasant green arbour in summer. Underneath are three metal chairs and matching table, bearing traces of white paint, which – like the green brocade curtains, the picture of the horse with orange mane, the poles, chicken wire and vines – have been discarded by the various employers for whom Moreke works in the city as an itinerant gardener. The arbour is between the garage and the lavatory, which is shared by everyone on the property, both tenants and lodgers.

On Sundays Moreke sits under his grapevine and drinks a bottle of beer brought from the shebeen across the road. Even in winter he sits there; it is warmer out in the midday winter sun than in the house, the shadow of the vine merely a twisted rope – grapes eaten, roof of leaves fallen. Although the yard is behind the house and there is a yellow dog on guard tied to a packing-case shelter, there is not much privacy. A large portion of the space of the family living in the garage is taken up by a paraffin-powered refrigerator filled with soft-drink cans and pots of flavoured yoghurt: a useful little business that serves the community and supplements the earnings of the breadwinner, a cleaner at the city slaughter-house. The sliding metal shutter meant for the egress of a car from the garage is permanently bolted down. All day Sunday children come on errands to buy, knocking at the old kitchen door, salvaged from the city, that Moreke has set into the wall of the garage.

A street where there is a shebeen, a house opposite a shebeen cannot be private, anyway. All weekend drunks wander over the ruts that make the gait even of the sober seem drunken. The children playing in the street take no notice of men fuddled between song and argument, who talk to people who are not there.

As well as friends and relatives, acquaintances of Moreke who have got to know where he lives through travelling with him on the buses to work walk over from the shebeen and appear in the yard. He is a man who always puts aside money to buy the Sunday newspaper; he has to fold away the paper and talk instead. The guests usually bring a cold quart or two with them (the shebeen, too, has a paraffin refrigerator, restaurant-size). Talk and laughter make the dog bark. Someone plays a transistor radio. The chairs are filled and some comers stretch on the bit of tough grass. Most of the Sunday visitors are men but there are women, particularly young ones, who have gone with them to the shebeen or taken up with them there; these women are polite and deferential to Moreke's wife, Nanike, when she has time to join the gathering. Often they will hold her latest – fifth living – baby while she goes

3

back into the kitchen to cook or hangs her washing on the fence. She takes a beer or two herself, but although she is in her early thirties and knows she is still pretty – except for a missing front tooth – she does not get flirtatious or giggle. She is content to sit with the new baby on her lap, in the sun, among men and women like herself, while her husband tells anecdotes which make them laugh or challenge him. He learns a lot from the newspapers.

She was sitting in the yard with him and his friends the Sunday a cousin arrived with a couple of hangers-on. They didn't bring beer, but were given some. There were greetings, but who really hears names? One of the hangers-on fell asleep on the grass, a boy with a body like a baggy suit. The other had a yellow face, lighter than anyone else present, narrow as a trowel, and the irregular pock-marks of the pitted skin were flocked, round the area where men grow hair, with sparse tufts of black. She noticed he wore a gold ear-ring in one ear. He had nothing to say but later took up a guitar belonging to someone else and played to himself. One of the people living in the garage, crossing the path of the group under the arbour on his way to the lavatory with his roll of toilet paper, paused to look or listen, but everyone else was talking too loudly to hear the soft plang-plang, and after-buzz when the player's palm stilled the instrument's vibration.

Moreke went off with his friends when they left, and came back, not late. His wife had gone to bed. She was sleepy, feeding the baby. Because he stood there, at the foot of the bed, did not begin to undress, she understood someone must be with him.

'Mtembu's friend.' Her husband's head indicated the other side of the glass-paned door.

'What does he want here now?'

'I brought him. Mtembu asked.'

'What for?'

Moreke sat down on the bed. He spoke softly, mouthing at her face. 'He needs somewhere to stay.'

'Where was he before, then?'

Moreke lifted and dropped his elbows limply at a question not to be asked.

The baby lost the nipple and nuzzled furiously at air. She

4

guided its mouth. 'Why can't he stay with Mtembu? You could have told Mtembu no.'

'He's your cousin.'

'Well, I will tell him no. If Mtembu needs somewhere to stay, I have to take him. But not anyone he brings from the street.'

Her husband yawned, straining every muscle in his face. Suddenly he stooped and began putting together the sheets of his Sunday paper that were scattered on the floor. He folded them more or less in order, slapping and smoothing the creases.

'Well?'

He said nothing, walked out. She heard the voices in the kitchen, but not what was being said.

He opened their door again and shut it behind him. 'It's not a business of cousins. This one is in trouble. You don't read the papers . . . the blowing up of that police station . . . *you* know, last month? They didn't catch them all . . . It isn't safe for Mtembu to keep him any longer. He must keep moving.'

Her soft jowls stiffened.

Her husband assured her awkwardly. 'A few days. Only for a couple of days. Then – (a gesture) – out of the country.'


*He never takes off the gold ear-ring, even when he sleeps. He sleeps on the sofa. He didn't bring a blanket, a towel, nothing – uses our things. I don't know what the ear-ring means; when I was a child there were men who came to work on the mines who had ear-rings, but in both ears – country people. He's a town person; another one who reads newspapers. He tidies away the blankets I gave him and then he reads newspapers the whole day. He can't go out.*


The others at Number 1907 Block C were told the man was Nanike Moreke's cousin, had come to look for work and had nowhere to stay. There are people in that position in every house. No one with a roof over his head can say 'no' to one of the same

5

blood – everyone knows that; Moreke's wife had not denied that. But she wanted to know what to say if someone asked the man's name. He himself answered at once, his strong thin hand twisting the gold hoop in his ear like a girl. 'Shisonka. Tell them Shisonka.'

'And the other name?'

Her husband answered. 'That name is enough.'

Moreke and his wife didn't use the name among themselves. They referred to the man as 'he' and 'him'. Moreke addressed him as 'Mfo', brother; she called him simple 'you'. Moreke answered questions nobody asked. He said to his wife, in front of the man, 'What is the same blood? Here in this place? If you are not white, you are all the same blood, here.' She looked at her husband respectfully, as she did when he read to her out of his newspaper.

The woman lodger worked in the kitchen at a Kentucky Fried Chicken shop in the city, and like Moreke was out at work all day; at weekends she slept at her mother's place, where her children lived, so she did not know the man Shisonka never left the house to look for work or for any other reason. Her lover came to her room only to share the bed, creeping late past whatever sleeping form might be on the sofa, and leaving before first light to get to a factory in the white industrial area. The only problem was the family who lived in the garage. The man had to cross the yard to use the lavatory. The slaughter-house cleaner's mother and wife would notice he was there, in the house; that he never went out. It was Moreke's wife who thought of this, and told the woman in the garage her cousin was sick, he had just been discharged from hospital. And indeed, they took care of him as if he had been – Moreke and his wife Nanike. They did not have the money to eat meat often but on Tuesday Moreke bought a pluck from the butchery near the bus station in the city: the man sat down to eat with them. Moreke brought cigarettes home – the man paid him – it was clear he must have cigarettes, needed cigarettes more than food. And don't let him go out, don't ever let him go to the shop for cigarettes, or over to Ma Radebe for drink, Moreke told his wife, *you* go, if he needs anything, *you* just leave everything, shut the house – go.

6

*I wash his clothes with our things. His shirt and pullover have labels in another language, come from some other country. Even the letters that spell it are different. I give him food in the middle of the day. I myself eat in the yard, with the baby. I told him he should play the music, in there, if he wants to. He listens to Samson's tapes. How could I keep my own sister out of the house? When she saw him I said he was a friend of Samson – a new friend. She likes light-skinned. But it means people notice you. It must be very hard to hide. He doesn't say so. He doesn't look afraid. The beard will hide him; but how long does it take for a beard to grow, how long, how long before he goes away.*

Every night that week the two men talked. Not in the room with the sofa and radio-and-cassette-player, if the woman lodger was at home on the other side of the curtains, but in the room where the Morekes slept. The man had a kitchen chair Moreke brought in, there was just room for it between the big bed and the wardrobe. Moreke lay on the bed with a pillow stuffed under his nape. Sometimes his wife stayed in the kitchen, at other times she came in and sat with the baby on the bed. She could see Moreke's face and the back of the man's head in the panel mirror of the wardrobe while they talked. The shape of the head swelled up from the thin neck, a puff-ball of black kapok. Deep in, there was a small patch without hair, a skin infection or a healed wound. His front aspect – a narrow yellow face keenly attentive, cigarette wagging like a finger from the corner of his lips, loop of gold round the lobe of one of the alert pointed ears – seemed unaware of the blemish, something that attacked him unnoticed from behind.

They talked about the things that interested Moreke; the political meetings disguised as church services of which he read reports but did not attend. The man laughed, and argued with Moreke patiently. 'What's the use, man? If you don't stand there? Stand with your feet as well as agree with your head . . . Yes, go and get that head knocked if the dogs and the *kerries* come. Since '76, the kids've showed you how . . . You know now.'

Moreke wanted to tell the man what he thought of the Urban Councils the authorities set up, and the committees people themselves had formed in opposition, as, when he found himself in the company of a sports promoter, he wanted to give his opinion of the state of soccer today. 'Those council men are nothing to me. You understand? They only want big jobs and smart cars for themselves. I'm a poor man, I'll never have a car. But they say they're going to make this place like white Jo'burg. Maybe the government listens to them . . . They say they can do it. The committees – eh? – they say like *I* do, *those council men are nothing* – but they themselves, what can they do? They know everything is no good here. They talk; they tell about it; they go to jail. So what's the use? What can you do?'

The man did not tell what he had done. 'The police station' was there, ready in their minds, ready to their tongues, not spoken.

The man was smiling at Moreke, at something he had heard many times before and might be leaving behind for good, now. 'Your council. Those dummies. You see this *donga* called a street, outside? This place without even electric light in the rooms? You dig beautiful gardens, the flowers smell nice . . . and how many people must shit in that stinking hovel in your yard? How much do you get for digging the ground white people own? You told me what you get. "Top wages": ten rands a day. Just enough for the rent in this place, and not even the shit-house belongs to you, not even the mud you bring in from the yard on your shoes . . .'

Moreke became released, excited. 'The bus fares went up last week. They say the rent is going up . . .'

'Those dummies, that's what they do for you. You see? But the committee tells you don't pay that rent, because you aren't paid enough to live in the "beautiful city" the dummies promise you. Isn't that the truth? Isn't the truth what you *know*? Don't you listen to the ones who speak the truth?'

Moreke's wife had had, for a few minutes, the expression of one waiting to interrupt. 'I'll go to Radebe and get a bottle of beer, if you want.'

The two men gave a flitting nod to one another in approval.

Moreke counted out the money. 'Don't let anybody come back with you.'

His wife took the coins without looking up. 'I'm not a fool.' The baby was asleep on the bed. She closed the door quietly behind

8

her. The two men lost the thread of their talk for a moment; Moreke filled it: 'A good woman.'

*We are alone together. The baby likes him. I don't give the breast every time, now; yesterday when I was fetching the coal he fed the bottle to her. I ask him what children he has? He only smiles, shakes his head. I don't know if this means it was silly to ask, because everyone has children.*

*Perhaps it meant he doesn't know, pretends he doesn't know – thinks a lot of himself, smart young man with a gold ring in his ear has plenty of girl-friends to get babies with him.*

The police station was never mentioned, but the man spent one of the nights describing to the Moreke couple foreign places he had been to – that must have been before the police station happened. He told about the oldest city on the African continent, so old it had a city of the dead as well as a city of the living – a whole city of tombs like houses. The religion there was the same as the religion of the Indian shopkeepers, here at home. Then he had lived in another kind of country, where there was snow for half the year or more. It was dark until ten in the morning and again from three o'clock in the afternoon. He described the clothes he had been given to protect him against the cold. 'Such people, I can tell you. You can't believe such white people exist. If our people turn up there . . . you get everything you need they just give it . . . and there's a museum, it's out in the country, they have ships there their people sailed all over the world more than a thousand years ago. They may even have come here . . . This pullover is still from them . . . full of holes now . . .'

'Look at that, *hai!*' Moreke admired the intricately-worked bands of coloured wools in a design based upon natural features he did not recognise – dark frozen forms of fir forests and the constellation of snow crystals. 'She'll mend it for you.'

His wife was willing but apprehensive. 'I'll try and get the same colours. I don't know if I can find them here.'

9

The man smiled at the kindness of his own people. 'She shouldn't take a lot of trouble. I won't need it, anyway.'

No one asked where it was the pullover wouldn't be needed; what kind of place, what continent he would be going to when he got away.

After the man had retired to his sofa that night Moreke read the morning paper he had brought from an employer's kitchen in the city. He kept lowering the sheets slowly and looking around at the room, then returning to his reading. The baby was restless; but it was not that he commented on.

'It's better not to know too much about him.'

His wife turned the child onto its belly. 'Why?'

Her face was innocently before his like a mirror he didn't want to look into. He had kept encouraging the man to go on with his talk of living in foreign places.

The shadows thrown by the candle capered through the room, bending furniture and bodies, flying over the ceiling, quieting the baby with wonder. 'Because then . . . if they question us, we won't have anything to tell.'


*He did bring something. A gun.*

*He comes into the kitchen, now, and helps me when I'm washing up. He came in, this morning, and put his hands in the soapy water, didn't say anything, started cleaning up. Our hands were in the grease and soap, I couldn't see his fingers but sometimes I felt them when they bumped mine. He scraped the pot and dried everything. I didn't say thanks. To say thank you to a man – it's not man's work, he might feel ashamed.*

*He stays in the kitchen – we stay in the kitchen with the baby most of the day. He doesn't sit in there, anymore, listening to the tapes. I go and turn on the machine loud enough for us to hear it well in the kitchen.*


By Thursday the tufts of beard were thickening and knitting together on the man's face. Samson Moreke tried to find Mtembu to hear what plans had been made but Mtembu did not come in response to messages and was not anywhere Moreke looked for

10

him. Moreke took the opportunity, while the woman in whose garden he worked on Thursdays was out, to telephone Mtembu's place of work from her house, but was told that workshop employees were not allowed to receive calls.

He brought home chicken feet for soup and a piece of beef shank. Figs had ripened in the Thursday garden and he'd been given some in a newspaper poke. He asked, 'When do you expect to hear from Mtembu?'

The man was reading the sheet of paper stained with milky sap from the stems of figs. Samson Moreke had never really been in jail himself – only the usual short-term stays for pass offences – but he knew from people who had been inside a long time that there was this need to read every scrap of paper that might come your way from the outside world.

'– Well, it doesn't matter. You're all right here. We can just carry on. I suppose Mtembu will turn up this weekend.'

As if he heard in this resignation Moreke's anticipation of the usual Sunday beer in the yard, the man suddenly took charge of Moreke and his wife, crumpling the dirty newspaper and rubbing his palms together to rid them of stickiness. His narrow yellow face was set clear-cut in black hair all round now, like the framed face of the king in Moreke's worn pack of cards. The black eyes and ear-ring were the same liquid-bright. The perfectly-ironed shirt he wore was open at the breast in the manner of all attractive young men of his age. 'Look, nobody must come here. Saturday, Sunday. None of your friends. You must shut up this place. Keep them all away. Nobody walking into the yard from the shebeen. That's *out*.'

Moreke looked from the man to his wife; back to the man again. Moreke half-coughed, half-laughed. 'But how do I do that, man? How do I stop them? I can't put bars on my gate. There're the other people, in the garage. They sell things.'

'*You* stay inside. Here in this house, with the doors locked. There are too many people around at the weekend. Let them think you've gone away.'

Moreke still smiled, amazed, helpless. 'And the one in there, with her boy-friend? What's she going to think?'

Moreke's wife spoke swiftly. 'She'll be at her mother's house.'

11

And now the plan of action fell efficiently into place, each knew his part within it. 'Oh yes. Thank the Lord for that. Maybe I'll go over to Radebe's tonight and just say I'm not going to be here Sunday. And Saturday I'll say I'm going to the soccer.'

His wife shook her head. 'Not the soccer. Your friends will want to come and talk about it afterwards.'

'*Hai, mama!* All right, a funeral, far away . . .' Moreke laughed, and stopped himself with an embarrassed drawing of mucus back through the nose.

*While I'm ironing, he cleans the gun.*

*I saw he needed another rag and I gave it to him.*

*He asked for oil, and I took cooking oil out of the cupboard, but then I saw in his face that was not what he wanted. I went to the garage and borrowed Three-in-One from Nchaba's wife.*

*He never takes out the gun when Samson's here. He knows only he and I know about it.*

*I said, what happened there, on your head at the back – that sore. His hand went to it, under the hair, he doesn't think it shows. I'll get him something for it, some ointment. If he's still here on Monday.*

*Perhaps he is cross because I spoke about it.*

*Then when I came back with the oil, he sat at the kitchen table laughing at me, smiling, as if I was a young girl. I forgot – I felt I was a girl. But I don't really like that kind of face, his face – light-skinned. You can never forget a face like that. If you are questioned, you can never say you don't remember what someone like that looks like.*

*He picks up the baby as if it belongs to him. To him as well, while we are in the kitchen together.*

That night the two men didn't talk. They seemed to have nothing to say. Like prisoners who get their last mealie-pap of the day before being locked up for the night, Moreke's wife gave them their meal before dark. Then all three went from the kitchen to the Morekes' room, where any light that might shine from behind the curtains and give away a presence was directed only towards a

12

blind: a high corrugated tin fence in a lane full of breast-high khakiweed. Moreke shared his newspaper. When the man had read it, he tossed through third-hand adventure comics and the sales promotion pamphlets given away in city supermarkets Nanike Moreke kept; he read the manual 'Teach Yourself How to Sell Insurance' in which, at some stage, 'Samson Moreke' had been carefully written on the fly-leaf.

There was no beer. Moreke's wife knew her way about her kitchen in the dark; she fetched the litre bottle of coke that was on the kitchen table and poured herself a glass. Her husband stayed the offer with a raised hand; the other man's inertia over the manual was overcome just enough to move his head in refusal. She had taken up again the cover for the bed she had begun when she had had some free time, waiting for this fifth child to be born. Crocheted roses, each caught in a squared web of a looser pattern, were worked separately and then joined to the whole they slowly extended. The tiny flash of her steel hook and the hair-thin gold in his ear signalled in candlelight. At about ten o'clock there was a knock at the front door. The internal walls of these houses are planned at minimum specification for cheapness and a blow on any part of the house reverberates through every room. The black-framed, bone-yellow face raised and held, absolutely still, above the manual. Moreke opened his mouth and, swinging his legs over the side, lifted himself from the bed. But his wife's hand on his shoulder made him subside again; only the bed creaked slightly. The slenderness of her body from the waist up was merely rooted in heavy maternal hips and thighs; with a movement soft as the breath expelled, she leant and blew out the candles.

A sensible precaution; someone might follow round the walls of the house looking for some sign of life. They sat in the dark. There was no bark from the dog in the yard. The knocking stopped. Moreke thought he heard laughter, and the gate twang. But the shebeen is noisy on a Friday, the sounds could have come from anywhere. 'Just someone who's had a few drinks. It often happens. Sometimes we don't even wake up, I suppose, ay, Nanike.' Moreke's hoarse whisper, strangely, woke the baby, who let out the thin wail that meets the spectre in a bad dream, breaks through into consciousness against a threat that can't be defeated in the conscious world. In the dark, they all went to bed.

*A city of the dead, a city of the living. It was better when Samson got him to talk about things like that. Things far away can't do any harm. We'll never have a car, like the councillors, and we'll never have to run away to those far places, like him. Lucky to have this house; many, many people are jealous of that. I never knew, until this house was so quiet, how much noise people make at the weekend, I didn't hear the laughing, the talking in the street, Radebe's music going, the terrible screams of people fighting.*

On Saturday Moreke took his blue ruled pad and an envelope to the kitchen table. But his wife was peeling pumpkin and slicing onions, there was no space, so he went back to the room where the sofa was, and his radio-and-cassette-player. First he addressed the envelope to their twelve-year-old boy at mission school. It took him the whole morning to write a letter, although he could read so well. Once or twice he asked the man how to spell a word in English.

He lay smoking on his bed, the sofa. 'Why in English?'

'Rapula knows English very well . . . it helps him to get letters . . .'

'You shouldn't send him away from here, *baba*. You think it's safer, but you are wrong. It's like you and the meetings. The more you try to be safe, the worse it will be for your children.'

He stared quietly at Moreke. 'And look, now I'm here.'

'Yes.'

'And you look after me.'

'Yes.'

'And you're not afraid.'

'Yes, we're afraid . . . but of many things . . . when I come home with money . . . Three times tsotsis have hit me, taken everything. You see here where I was cut on the cheek. This arm was broken. I couldn't work. Not even push the lawnmower. I had to pay some young one to hold my jobs for me.'

14

The man smoked and smiled. 'I don't understand you. You see? I don't understand you. Bring your children home, man. We're shut up in the ghetto to kill each other. That's what they want, in their white city. So you send the children away; that's what they want, too. To get rid of us. We must all stick together. That's the only way to fight our way out.'

That night he asked if Moreke had a chess set.

Moreke giggled, gave clucks of embarrassment. 'That board with the little dolls? I'm not an educated man! I don't know those games!'

They played together the game that everybody knows, that is played on the pavements outside shops and in factory yards, with the board drawn on concrete or in dust, and bottle-tops for counters. This time a handful of dried beans from the kitchen served, and a board drawn by Moreke on a box-lid. He won game after game from the man. His wife had the Primus stove in the room, now, and she made tea. The game was not resumed. She had added three completed squares to her bed-cover in two nights; after the tea, she did not take it up again. They sat listening to Saturday night, all round them, pressing in upon the hollow cement units of which the house was built. Often tramping steps seemed just about to halt at the front or back door. The splintering of wood under a truncheon or the shatter of the window-panes, thin ice under the weight of the roving dark outside, waited upon every second. The woman's eyelids slid down, fragile and faintly greasy, outlining intimately the aspect of the orbs beneath, in sleep. Her face became unguarded as the baby's. Every now and then she would start, come to herself again. But her husband and the man made no move to go to bed. The man picked up and ran the fine head of her crochet hook under the rind of each fingernail, again and again, until the tool had done the cleaning job to satisfaction.

When the man went to bed at last, by the light of the cigarette lighter he shielded in his hand to see his way to the sofa, he found she had put a plastic chamber-pot on the floor. Probably the husband had thought of it.

All Sunday morning the two men worked together on a fault in

15

Moreke's tape-player, though they were unable to test it with the volume switched on. Moreke could not afford to take the player to a repair shop. The man seemed to think the fault a simple matter; like any other city youngster, he had grown up with such machines. Moreke's wife cooked mealie-rice and made a curry gravy for the Sunday meal. 'Should I go to Radebe and get beer?' She had followed her husband into their room to ask him alone.

'You want to advertise we are here? You know what he said.'

'Ask him if it matters, if I go – a woman.'

'I'm not going to ask. Did he say he wants beer? Did I?'

But in the afternoon she did ask something. She went straight to the man, not Moreke. 'I have to go out to the shop.' It was very hot in the closed house; the smell of curry mixed with the smell of the baby in the fug of its own warmth and wrappings. He wrinkled his face, exposed clenched teeth in a suppressed yawn; what shops – had she forgotten it was Sunday? She understood his reaction. But there were corner shops that sold essentials even on Sundays; he must know that. 'I have to get milk. Milk for the baby.'

She stood there, in her over-trodden slippers, her old skirt and cheap blouse – a woman not to be noticed among every other woman in the streets. He didn't refuse her. No need. Not after all this past week. Not for the baby. She was not like her husband, big-mouth, friendly with everyone. He nodded; it was a humble errand that wouldn't concern him.

She went out of the house just as she was, her money in her hand. Moreke and the baby were asleep in their room. The street looked new, bright, refreshing, after the dim house. A small boy with a toy machine-gun covered her in his fire, chattering his little white teeth with rat-a-tat-tttt. Ma Radebe, the shebeen-keeper, her hair plaited with blue and red beads, her beautiful long red nails resting on the steering wheel, was backing her car out of her gateway. She braked to let her neighbour pass and leaned from the car window. '*My dear* (in English), I was supposed to be gone from this place two hours ago. I'm due at a big wedding that will already be over . . . How are you? Didn't see your husband for a few days . . . nothing wrong across the road?'

Moreke's wife stood and shook her head. Radebe was not one

16

who expected or waited for answers when she greeted anyone. When the car had driven off Moreke's wife went on down the street and down the next one, past the shop where young boys were gathered scuffling and dancing to the shopkeeper's radio, and on to the purplish brick building with the security fence round it and a flag flying. One of her own people was on guard outside, lolling with a sub-machine-gun. She went up the steps and into the office, where there were more of her own people in uniform, but one of *them* in charge. She spoke in her own language to her own kind, but they seemed disbelieving. They repeated the name of that other police station, that was blown up, and asked her if she was sure? She said she was quite sure. Then they took her to the white officer and she told in English – 'There, in my house, 1907 Block C. He has been there a week. He has a gun.'

*I don't know why I did it. I get ready to say that to anyone who is going to ask me, but nooody in this house asks. The baby laughs at me while I wash her, stares up while we're alone in the house and she's feeding at the breast, and to her I say out loud: I don't know why.*

A week after the man was taken away that Sunday by the security police, Ma Radebe again met Moreke's wife in their street. The shebeen-keeper gazed at her for a moment, and spat.

17

# Country Lovers

The farm children play together when they are small; but once the white children go away to school they soon don't play together any more, even in the holidays. Although most of the black children get some sort of schooling, they drop every year further behind the grades passed by the white children; the childish vocabulary, the child's exploration of the adventurous possibilities of dam, koppies, mealie lands and veld – there comes a time when the white children have surpassed these with the vocabulary of boarding-school and the possibilities of inter-school sports matches and the kind of adventures seen at the cinema. This usefully coincides with the age of twelve or thirteen; so that by the time early adolescence is reached, the black children are making, along with the bodily changes common to all, an easy transition to adult forms of address, beginning to call their old playmates *missus* and *baasie* – little master.

The trouble was Paulus Eysendyck did not seem to realise that Thebedi was now simply one of the crowd of farm children down at the kraal, recognisable in his sisters' old clothes. The first Christmas holidays after he had gone to boarding-school he brought home for Thebedi a painted box he had made in his wood-work class. He had to give it to her secretly because he had nothing for the other children at the kraal. And she gave him, before he went back to school, a bracelet she had made of thin brass wire and the grey-and-white beans of the castor-oil crop his father cultivated. (When they used to play together, she was the one who had taught Paulus how to make clay oxen for their toy spans.) There was a craze, even in the *platteland* towns like the one where he was at school, for boys to wear elephant-hair and other bracelets beside their watch-straps; his was admired, friends

18

asked him to get similar ones for them. He said the natives made them on his father's farm and he would try.

When he was fifteen, six feet tall, and tramping round at school dances with the girls from the 'sister' school in the same town; when he had learnt how to tease and flirt and fondle quite intimately these girls who were the daughters of prosperous farmers like his father; when he had even met one who, at a wedding he had attended with his parents on a nearby farm, had let him do with her in a locked storeroom what people did when they made love – when he was as far from his childhood as all this, he still brought home from a shop in town a red plastic belt and gilt hoop ear-rings for the black girl, Thebedi. She told her father the missus had given these to her as a reward for some work she had done – it was true she sometimes was called to help out in the farmhouse. She told the girls in the kraal that she had a sweetheart nobody knew about, far away, away on another farm, and they giggled, and teased, and admired her. There was a boy in the kraal called Njabulo who said he wished he could have bought her a belt and ear-rings.

When the farmer's son was home for the holidays she wandered far from the kraal and her companions. He went for walks alone. They had not arranged this; it was an urge each followed independently. He knew it was she, from a long way off. She knew that his dog would not bark at her. Down at the dried-up river-bed where five or six years ago the children had caught a leguaan one great day – a creature that combined ideally the size and ferocious aspect of the crocodile with the harmlessness of the lizard – they squatted side by side on the earth bank. He told her traveller's tales: about school, about the punishments at school, particularly, exaggerating both their nature and his indifference to them. He told her about the town of Middleburg, which she had never seen. She had nothing to tell but she prompted with many questions, like any good listener. While he talked he twisted and tugged at the roots of white stinkwood and Cape willow trees that looped out of the eroded earth around them. It had always been a good spot for children's games, down there hidden by the mesh of old, ant-eaten trees held in place by vigorous ones, wild asparagus bushing

19

up between the trunks, and here and there prickly-pear cactus sunken-skinned and bristly, like an old man's face, keeping alive sapless until the next rainy season. She punctured the dry hide of a prickly-pear again and again with a sharp stick while she listened. She laughed a lot at what he told her, sometimes dropping her face on her knees, sharing amusement with the cool shady earth beneath her bare feet. She put on her pair of shoes – white sandals, thickly Blanco-ed against the farm dust – when he was on the farm, but these were taken off and laid aside, at the river-bed.

One summer afternoon when there was water flowing there and it was very hot she waded in as they used to do when they were children, her dress bunched modestly and tucked into the legs of her pants. The schoolgirls he went swimming with at dams or pools on neighbouring farms wore bikinis but the sight of their dazzling bellies and thighs in the sunlight had never made him feel what he felt now, when the girl came up the bank and sat beside him, the drops of water beading off her dark legs the only points of light in the earth-smelling, deep shade. They were not afraid of one another, they had known one another always; he did with her what he had done that time in the storeroom at the wedding, and this time it was so lovely, so lovely, he was surprised . . . and she was surprised by it, too – he could see in her dark face that was part of the shade, with her big dark eyes, shiny as soft water, watching him attentively: as she had when they used to huddle over their teams of mud oxen, as she had when he told her about detention weekends at school.

They went to the river-bed often through those summer holidays. They met just before the light went, as it does quite quickly, and each returned home with the dark – she to her mother's hut, he to the farmhouse – in time for the evening meal. He did not tell her about school or town any more. She did not ask questions any longer. He told her, each time, when they would meet again. Once or twice it was very early in the morning; the lowing of the cows being driven to graze came to them where they lay, dividing them with unspoken recognition of the sound read in their two pairs of eyes, opening so close to each other.

He was a popular boy at school. He was in the second, then the

20

first soccer team. The head girl of the 'sister' school was said to have a crush on him; he didn't particularly like her, but there was a pretty blonde who put up her long hair into a kind of doughnut with a black ribbon round it, whom he took to see films when the schoolboys and girls had a free Saturday afternoon. He had been driving tractors and other farm vehicles since he was ten years old, and as soon as he was eighteen he got a driver's licence and in the holidays, this last year of his school life, he took neighbours' daughters to dances and to the drive-in cinema that had just opened twenty kilometres from the farm. His sisters were married, by then; his parents often left him in charge of the farm over the weekend while they visited the young wives and grandchildren.

When Thebedi saw the farmer and his wife drive away on a Saturday afternoon, the boot of their Mecedes filled with fresh-killed poultry and vegetables from the garden that it was part of her father's work to tend, she knew that she must come not to the river-bed but up to the house. The house was an old one, thick-walled, dark against the heat. The kitchen was its lively thorough-fare, with servants, food supplies, begging cats and dogs, pots boiling over, washing being damped for ironing, and the big deep-freeze the missus had ordered from town, bearing a crocheted mat and a vase of plastic irises. But the dining-room with the bulging-legged heavy table was shut up in its rich, old smell of soup and tomato sauce. The sitting-room curtains were drawn and the T.V. set silent. The door of the parents' bedroom was locked and the empty rooms where the girls had slept had sheets of plastic spread over the beds. It was in one of these that she and the farmer's son stayed together whole nights – almost: she had to get away before the house servants, who knew her, came in at dawn. There was a risk someone would discover her or traces of her presence if he took her to his own bedroom, although she had looked into it many times when she was helping out in the house and knew well, there, the row of silver cups he had won at school.

When she was eighteen and the farmer's son nineteen and working with his father on the farm before entering a veterinary college, the young man Njabulo asked her father for her. Njabulo's parents met with hers and the money he was to pay in place of the cows it is customary to give a prospective bride's parents was settled upon. He had no cows to offer; he was a labourer on the Eysendyck farm, like her father. A bright youngster; old Eysendyck had taught him brick-laying and was using him for odd jobs in construction, around the place. She did not tell the farmer's son that her parents had arranged for her to marry. She did not tell him, either, before he left for his first term at the veterinary college, that she thought she was going to have a baby. Two months after her marriage to Njabulo, she gave birth to a daughter. There was no disgrace in that; among her people it is customary for a young man to make sure, before marriage, that the chosen girl is not barren, and Njabulo had made love to her then. But the infant was very light and did not quickly grow darker as most African babies do. Already at birth there was on its head a quantity of straight, fine floss, like that which carries the seeds of certain weeds in the veld. The unfocused eyes it opened were grey flecked with yellow. Njabulo was the matt, opaque coffee-grounds colour that has always been called black; the colour of Thebedi's legs on which beaded water looked oyster-shell blue, the same colour as Thebedi's face, where the black eyes, with their interested gaze and clear whites, were so dominant.

Njabulo made no complaint. Out of his farm labourer's earnings he bought from the Indian store a cellophane-windowed pack containing a pink plastic bath, six napkins, a card of safety pins, a knitted jacket, cap and bootees, a dress, and a tin of Johnson's Baby Powder, for Thebedi's baby.

When it was two weeks old Paulus Eysendyck arrived home from the veterinary college for the holidays. He drank a glass of fresh, still-warm milk in the childhood familiarity of his mother's kitchen and heard her discussing with the old house-servant where they could get a reliable substitute to help out now that the girl Thebedi had had a baby. For the first time since he was a small boy he came right into the kraal. It was eleven o'clock in the morning. The men were at work in the lands. He looked about him, urgently; the women turned away, each not wanting to be the one approached to point out where Thebedi lived. Thebedi appeared, coming slowly from the hut Njabulo had built in white man's style, with a tin chimney, and a proper window with glass panes set in straight as walls made of unfired bricks would allow. She greeted him with hands brought together and a token movement representing the respectful bob with which she was accustomed to acknowledge she was in the presence of his father or mother. He lowered his head under the doorway of her home and went in. He said, 'I want to see. Show me.'

She had taken the bundle off her back before she came out into the light to face him. She moved between the iron bedstead made up with Njabulo's checked blankets and the small wooden table where the pink plastic bath stood among food and kitchen pots, and picked up the bundle from the snugly-blanketed grocer's box where it lay. The infant was asleep; she revealed the closed, pale, plump tiny face, with a bubble of spit at the corner of the mouth, the spidery pink hands stirring. She took off the woollen cap and the straight fine hair flew up after it in static electricity, showing gilded strands here and there. He said nothing. She was watching him as she had done when they were little, and the gang of children had trodden down a crop in their games or transgressed in some other way for which he, as the farmer's son, the white one among them, must intercede with the farmer. She disturbed the sleeping face by scratching or tickling gently at a cheek with one finger, and slowly the eyes opened, saw nothing, were still asleep, and then, awake, no longer narrowed, looked out at them, grey with yellowish flecks, his own hazel eyes.

He struggled for a moment with a grimace of tears, anger and self-pity. She could not put out her hand to him. He said, 'You haven't been near the house with it?'

She shook her head.

'Never?'

Again she shook her head.

'Don't take it out. Stay inside. Can't you take it away some-where? You must give it to someone – '

She moved to the door with him.

He said, 'I'll see what I will do. I don't know.' And then he said: 'I feel like killing myself.'

Her eyes began to glow, to thicken with tears. For a moment

23

there was the feeling between them that used to come when they were alone down at the river-bed.

He walked out.

Two days later, when his mother and father had left the farm for the day, he appeared again. The women were away on the lands, weeding, as they were employed to do as casual labour in summer; only the very old remained, propped up on the ground outside the huts in the flies and the sun. Thebedi did not ask him in. The child had not been well; it had diarrhoea. He asked where its food was. She said, 'The milk comes from me.' He went into Njabulo's house, where the child lay; she did not follow but stayed outside the door and watched without seeing an old crone who had lost her mind, talking to herself, talking to the fowls who ignored her.

She thought she heard small grunts from the hut, the kind of infant grunt that indicates a full stomach, a deep sleep. After a time, long or short she did not know, he came out and walked away with plodding stride (his father's gait) out of sight, towards his father's house.

The baby was not fed during the night and although she kept telling Njabulo it was sleeping, he saw for himself in the morning that it was dead. He comforted her with words and caresses. She did not cry but simply sat, staring at the door. Her hands were cold as dead chickens' feet to his touch.

Njabulo buried the little baby where farm workers were buried, in the place in the veld the farmer had given them. Some of the mounds had been left to weather away unmarked, others were covered with stones and a few had fallen wooden crosses. He was going to make a cross but before it was finished the police came and dug up the grave and took away the dead baby: someone – one of the other labourers? their women? – had reported that the baby was almost white, that, strong and healthy, it had died suddenly after a visit by the farmer's son. Pathological tests on the infant corpse showed intestinal damage not always consistent with death by natural causes.

Thebedi went for the first time to the country town where Paulus had been to school, to give evidence at the preparatory examination into the charge of murder brought against him. She

24

cried hysterically in the witness box, saying yes, yes (the gilt hoop ear-rings swung in her ears), she saw the accused pouring liquid into the baby's mouth. She said he had threatened to shoot her if she told anyone.

More than a year went by before, in that same town, the case was brought to trial. She came to court with a new-born baby on her back. She wore gilt hoop ear-rings; she was calm, she said she had not seen what the white man did in the house.

Paulus Eysendyck said he had visited the hut but had not poisoned the child.

The defence did not contest that there had been a love relationship between the accused and the girl, or that intercourse had taken place, but submitted there was no proof that the child was the accused's.

The judge told the accused there was strong suspicion against him but not enough proof that he had committed the crime. The court could not accept the girl's evidence because it was clear she had committed perjury either at this trial or at the preparatory examination. There was the suggestion in the mind of the court that she might be an accomplice in the crime; but, again, insufficient proof.

The judge commended the honourable behaviour of the husband (sitting in court in a brown-and-yellow-quartered golf cap bought for Sundays) who had not rejected his wife and had 'even provided clothes for the unfortunate infant out of his slender means'.

The verdict on the accused was 'not guilty'.

The young white man refused to accept the congratulations of press and public and left the court with his mother's raincoat shielding his face from photographers. His father said to the press, 'I will try and carry on as best I can to hold up my head in the district.'

Interviewed by the Sunday papers, who spelled her name in a variety of ways, the black girl, speaking in her own language, was quoted beneath her photograph: 'It was a thing of our childhood, we don't see each other any more.'

# A Soldier's Embrace

The day the cease-fire was signed she was caught in a crowd. Peasant boys from Europe who had made up the colonial army and freedom fighters whose column had marched into town were staggering about together outside the barracks, not three blocks from her house in whose rooms, for ten years, she had heard the blurred parade-ground bellow of colonial troops being trained to kill and be killed.

The men weren't drunk. They linked and swayed across the street; because all that had come to a stop, everything *had* to come to a stop: they surrounded cars, bicycles, vans, nannies with children, women with loaves of bread or basins of mangoes on their heads, a road gang with picks and shovels, a Coca-Cola truck, an old man with a barrow who bought bottles and bones. They were grinning and laughing amazement. That it could be: there they were, bumping into each other's bodies in joy, looking into each other's rough faces, all eyes crescent-shaped, brimming greeting. The words were in languages not mutually comprehensible, but the cries were new, a whooping and crowing all understood. She was bumped and jostled and she let go, stopped trying to move in any self-determined direction. There were two soldiers in front of her, blocking her off by their clumsy embrace (how do you do it, how do you do what you've never done before) and the embrace opened like a door and took her in – a pink hand with bitten nails grasping her right arm, a black hand with a big-dialled watch and thong bracelet pulling at her left elbow. Their three heads collided gaily, musk of sweat and tang of strong sweet soap clapped a mask to her nose and mouth. They all gasped with delicious shock. They were saying things to each other. She put up an arm round each neck, the rough pile of an army haircut on one

26

side, the soft negro hair on the other, and kissed them both on the cheek. The embrace broke. The crowd wove her away behind backs, arms, jogging heads; she was returned to and took up the will of her direction again – she was walking home from the post office, where she had just sent a telegram to relatives abroad: ALL CALM DON'T WORRY.

The lawyer came back early from his offices because the courts were not sitting although the official celebration holiday was not until next day. He described to his wife the rally before the Town Hall, which he had watched from the office-building balcony. One of the guerilla leaders (not the most important; he on whose head the biggest price had been laid would not venture so soon and deep into the territory so newly won) had spoken for two hours from the balcony of the Town Hall. 'Brilliant. Their jaws dropped. Brilliant. They've never heard anything on that level: precise, reasoned – none of them would ever have believed it possible, out of the bush. You should have seen de Poorteer's face. He'd like to be able to get up and open his mouth like that. And be listened to like that . . .' The governor's handicap did not even bring the sympathy accorded to a stammer; he paused and gulped between words. The blacks had always used a portmanteau name for him that meant the-crane-who-is-trying-to-swallow-the-bullfrog.

One of the members of the black underground organisation that could now come out in brass-band support of the freedom fighters had recognised the lawyer across from the official balcony and given him the freedom fighters' salute. The lawyer joked about it, miming, full of pride. 'You should have been there – should have seen him, up there in the official party. I told you – really – you ought to have come to town with me this morning.'

'And what did you do?' She wanted to assemble all details.

'Oh I gave the salute in return, chaps in the street saluted *me* . . . everybody was doing it. *It was marvellous*. And the police standing by; just to think, last month – only last week – you'd have been arrested.'

'Like thumbing your nose at them,' she said, smiling.

27

'Did anything go on around here?'

'Muchanga was afraid to go out all day. He wouldn't even run up to the post office for me!' Their servant had come to them many years ago, from service in the house of her father, a colonial official in the Treasury.

'But there was no excitement?'

She told him: 'The soldiers and some freedom fighters mingled outside the barracks. I got caught for a minute or two. They were dancing about; you couldn't get through. All very good-natured. – Oh, I sent the cable.'


An accolade, one side a white cheek, the other a black. The white one she kissed on the left cheek, the black one on the right cheek, as if these were two sides of one face.

That vision, version, was like a poster; the sort of thing that was soon peeling off dirty shopfronts and bus shelters while the months of wrangling talks preliminary to the take-over by the black government went by.

To begin with, the cheek was not white but pale or rather sallow, the poor boy's pallor of winter in Europe (that draft must have only just arrived and not yet seen service) with homesick pimples sliced off by the discipline of an army razor. And the cheek was not black but opaque peat-dark, waxed with sweat round the plump contours of the nostril. As if she could return to the moment again, she saw what she had not consciously noted: there had been a narrow pink strip in the darkness near the ear, the sort of tender stripe of healed flesh revealed when a scab is nicked off a little before it is ripe. The scab must have come away that morning: the young man picked at it in the troop carrier or truck (whatever it was the freedom fighters had; the colony had been told for years that they were supplied by the Chinese and Russians indiscriminately) on the way to enter the capital in triumph.

According to newspaper reports, the day would have ended for the two young soldiers in drunkenness and whoring. She was, apparently, not yet too old to belong to the soldier's embrace of all that a land-mine in the bush might have exploded for ever. That

28

was one version of the incident. Another: the opportunity taken by a woman not young enough to be clasped in the arms of the one who (same newspaper, while the war was on, expressing the fears of the colonists for their women) would be expected to rape her.

She considered this version.

She had not kissed on the mouth, she had not sought anonymous lips and tongues in the licence of festival. Yet she had kissed. Watching herself again, she knew that. She had – god knows why – kissed them on either cheek, his left, his right. It was deliberate, if a swift impulse: she had distinctly made the move.

She did not tell what happened not because her husband would suspect licence in her, but because he would see her – born and brought up in the country as the daughter of an enlightened white colonial official, married to a white liberal lawyer well known for his defence of blacks in political trials – as giving free expression to liberal principles.

She had not told, she did not know what had happened.

She thought of a time long ago when a school camp had gone to the sea and immediately on arrival everyone had run down to the beach from the train, tripping and tearing over sand dunes of wild fig, aghast with ecstatic shock at the meeting with the water.


De Poorteer was recalled and the lawyer remarked to one of their black friends, 'The crane has choked on the bullfrog. I hear that's what they're saying in the Quarter.'

The priest who came from the black slum that had always been known simply by that anonymous term did not respond with any sort of glee. His reserve implied it was easy to celebrate; there were people who 'shouted freedom too loud all of a sudden'.

The lawyer and his wife understood: Father Mulumbua was one who had shouted freedom when it was dangerous to do so, and gone to prison several times for it, while certain people, now on the Interim Council set up to run the country until the new government took over, had kept silent. He named a few, but reluctantly. Enough to confirm their own suspicions – men who perhaps had made some deal with the colonial power to place its interests first, no matter what sort of government might emerge from the new constitution? Yet when the couple plunged into discussion their friend left them talking to each other while he drank his beer and gazed, frowning as if at a headache or because the sunset light hurt his eyes behind his spectacles, round her huge-leaved tropical plants that bowered the terrace in cool humidity.

They had always been rather proud of their friendship with him, this man in a cassock who wore a clenched fist carved of local ebony as well as a silver cross round his neck. His black face was habitually stern – a high seriousness balanced by sudden splurting laughter when they used to tease him over the fist – but never inattentively ill-at-ease.

'What was the matter?' She answered herself; 'I had the feeling he didn't want to come here.' She was using a paper handkerchief dipped in gin to wipe greenfly off the back of a pale new leaf that had shaken itself from its folds like a cut-out paper lantern.

'Good lord, he's been here hundreds of times.'

' – Before, yes.'


What things were they saying?

With the shouting in the street and the swaying of the crowd, the sweet powerful presence that confused the senses so that sound, sight, stink (sweat, cheap soap) ran into one tremendous sensation, she could not make out words that came so easily.

Not even what she herself must have said.


A few wealthy white men who had been boastful in their support of the colonial war and knew they would be marked down by the blacks as arch exploiters, left at once. Good riddance, as the lawyer and his wife remarked. Many ordinary white people who had lived contentedly, without questioning its actions, under the colonial government, now expressed an enthusiastic intention to help build a nation, as the newspapers put it. The lawyer's wife's neighbourhood butcher was one. 'I don't mind blacks.' He was expansive with her, in his shop that he had occupied for twelve years on a licence available only to white people. 'Makes no difference to me who you are so long as you're honest.' Next to a chart showing a beast mapped according to the cuts of meat it provided, he had hung a picture of the most important leader of the freedom fighters, expected to be first president. People like the butcher turned out with their babies clutching pennants when the leader drove through the town from the airport.

There were incidents (newspaper euphemism again) in the Quarter. It was to be expected. Political factions, tribally based, who had not fought the war, wanted to share power with the freedom fighters' party. Muchanga no longer went down to the Quarter on his day off. His friends came to see him and sat privately on their hunkers near the garden compost heap. The ugly mansions of the rich who had fled stood empty on the bluff above the sea, but it was said they would make money out of them yet – they would be bought as ambassadorial residences when independence came, and with it many black and yellow diplomats. Zealots who claimed they belonged to the Party burned shops and houses of the poorer whites who lived, as the lawyer said, 'in the inevitable echelon of colonial society', closest to the Quarter. A house in the lawyer's street was noticed by his wife to be accommodating what was certainly one of those families, in the outhouses; green nylon curtains had appeared at the garage windows, she reported. The suburb was pleasantly overgrown and well-to-do; no one rich, just white professional people and professors from the university. The barracks was empty now, except for an old man with a stump and a police uniform stripped of insignia, a friend of Muchanga, it turned out, who sat on a beer-crate at the gates. He had lost his job as night-watchman when one of the rich people went away, and was glad to have work.

The street had been perfectly quiet; except for that first day.


The fingernails she sometimes still saw clearly were bitten down until embedded in a thin line of dirt all round, in the pink blunt fingers. The thumb and thick fingertips were turned back coarsely

31

even while grasping her. Such hands had never been allowed to take possession. They were permanently raw, so young, from unloading coal, digging potatoes from the frozen Northern Hemisphere, washing hotel dishes. He had not been killed, and now that day of the cease-fire was over he would be delivered back across the sea to the docks, the stony farm, the scullery of the grand hotel. He would have to do anything he could get. There was unemployment in Europe where he had returned, the army didn't need all the young men any more.

A great friend of the lawyer and his wife, Chipande, was coming home from exile. They heard over the radio he was expected, accompanying the future president as confidential secretary, and they waited to hear from him.

The lawyer put up his feet on the empty chair where the priest had sat, shifting it to a comfortable position by hooking his toes, free in sandals, through the slats. 'Imagine, Chipande!' Chipande had been almost a protégé – but they didn't like the term, it smacked of patronage. Tall, cocky, casual Chipande, a boy from the slummiest part of the Quarter, was recommended by the White Fathers' Mission (was it by Father Mulumbua himself? – the lawyer thought so, his wife was not sure they remembered correctly). A bright kid who wanted to be articled to a lawyer. That was asking a lot, in those days – nine years ago. He never finished his apprenticeship because while he and his employer were soon close friends, and the kid picked up political theories from the books in the house he made free of, he became so involved in politics that he had to skip the country one jump ahead of a detention order signed by the crane-who-was-trying-to-swallow-the-bullfrog.

After two weeks, the lawyer phoned the offices the guerilla-movement-become-Party had set up openly in the town but apparently Chipande had an office in the former colonial secretariat. There he had a secretary of his own; he wasn't easy to reach. The lawyer left a message. The lawyer and his wife saw from the newspaper pictures he hadn't changed much: he had a beard and had adopted the Muslim cap favoured by political circles in exile on the East Coast.

He did come to the house eventually. He had the distracted, insistent friendliness of one who had no time to re-establish intimacy; it must be taken as read. And it must not be displayed. When he remarked on a shortage of accommodation for exiles now become officials, and the lawyer said the house was far too big for two people, he was welcome to move in and regard a self-contained part of it as his private living quarters, he did not answer but went on talking generalities. The lawyer's wife mentioned Father Mulumbua, whom they had not seen since just after the cease-fire. The lawyer added, 'There's obviously some sort of big struggle going on, he's fighting for his political life there in the Quarter.' 'Again,' she said, drawing them into a reminder of what had only just become their past.

But Chipande was restlessly following with his gaze the movements of old Muchanga, dragging the hose from plant to plant, careless of the spray; 'You remember who this is, Muchanga?' she had said when the visitor arrived, yet although the old man had given, in their own language, the sort of respectful greeting even an elder gives a young man whose clothes and bearing denote rank and authority, he was not in any way overwhelmed nor enthusiastic – perhaps he secretly supported one of the rival factions?

The lawyer spoke of the latest whites to leave the country – people who had got themselves quickly involved in the sort of currency swindle that draws more outrage than any other kind of crime, in a new state fearing the flight of capital: 'Let them go, let them go. Good riddance.' And he turned to talk of other things – there were so many more important questions to occupy the attention of the three old friends.

But Chipande couldn't stay. Chipande could not stay for supper; his beautiful long velvety black hands with their pale lining (as she thought of the palms) hung impatiently between his knees while he sat forward in the chair, explaining, adamant against persuasion. He should not have been there, even now; he had official business waiting, sometimes he drafted correspondence until one or two in the morning. The lawyer remarked how there hadn't been a proper chance to talk; he wanted to discuss those fellows in the Interim Council Mulumbua was so warily distrustful of – what did Chipande know?

Chipande, already on his feet, said something dismissing and very slightly disparaging, not about the council members but of Mulumbua – a reference to his connection with the Jesuit missionaries as an influence that 'comes through'. 'But I must make a note to see him sometime.'

It seemed that even black men who presented a threat to the Party could be discussed only among black men themselves, now. Chipande put an arm round each of his friends as for the brief official moment of a photograph, left them; he who used to sprawl on the couch arguing half the night before dossing down in the lawyer's pyjamas. 'As soon as I'm settled I'll contact you. You'll be around, ay?'

'Oh we'll be around.' The lawyer laughed, referring, for his part, to those who were no longer. 'Glad to see you're not driving a Mercedes!' he called with reassured affection at the sight of Chipande getting into a modest car. How many times, in the old days, had they agreed on the necessity for African leaders to live simply when they came to power!

On the terrace to which he turned back, Muchanga was doing something extraordinary – wetting a dirty rag with Gilbey's. It was supposed to be his day off, anyway; why was he messing about with the plants when one wanted peace to talk undisturbed?

'Is those thing again, those thing is killing the leaves.'

'For heaven's sake, he could use methylated for that! Any kind of alcohol will do! Why don't you get him some?'

There were shortages of one kind and another in the country, and gin happened to be something in short supply.


Whatever the hand had done in the bush had not coarsened it. It, too, was suède-black, and elegant. The pale lining was hidden against her own skin where the hand grasped her left elbow.

Strangely, black does not show toil – she remarked this as one remarks the quality of a fabric. The hand was not as long but as distinguished by beauty as Chipande's. The watch a fine piece of equipment for a fighter. There was something next to it, in fact looped over the strap by the angle of the wrist as the hand grasped. A bit of thong with a few beads knotted where it was joined as a bracelet. Or amulet. Their babies wore such things; often their first and only garment. Grandmothers or mothers attached it as protection. It had worked; he was alive at cease-fire. Some had been too deep in the bush to know, and had been killed after the fighting was over. He had pumped his head wildly and laughingly at whatever it was she – they – had been babbling.

The lawyer had more free time than he'd ever remembered. So many of his clients had left; he was deputed to collect their rents and pay their taxes for them, in the hope that their property wasn't going to be confiscated – there had been alarmist rumours among such people since the day of the cease-fire. But without the rich whites there was little litigation over possessions, whether in the form of the children of dissolved marriages or the houses and cars claimed by divorced wives. The Africans had their own ways of resolving such redistribution of goods. And a gathering of elders under a tree was sufficient to settle a dispute over boundaries or argue for and against the guilt of a woman accused of adultery. He had had a message, in a round-about way, that he might be asked to be consultant on constitutional law to the Party, but nothing seemed to come of it. He took home with him the proposals for the draft constitution he had managed to get hold of. He spent whole afternoons in his study making notes for counter- or improved proposals he thought he would send to Chipande or one of the other people he knew in high positions: every time he glanced up, there through his open windows was Muchanga's little company at the bottom of the garden. Once, when he saw they had straggled off, he wandered down himself to clear his head (he got drowsy, as he never did when he used to work twelve hours a day at the office). They ate dried shrimps, from the market: that's what they

35

were doing! The ground was full of bitten-off heads and black eyes on stalks. His wife smiled.

'They bring them. Muchanga won't go near the market since the riot.'

'It's ridiculous. Who's going to harm him?'

There was even a suggestion that the lawyer might apply for a professorship at the university. The chair of the Faculty of Law was vacant, since the students had demanded the expulsion of certain professors engaged during the colonial regime – in particular of the fuddy-duddy (good riddance) who had gathered dust in the Law chair, and the quite decent young man (pity about him) who had had Political Science. But what professor of Political Science could expect to survive both a colonial regime and the revolutionary regime that defeated it? The lawyer and his wife decided that since he might still be appointed in some consultative capacity to the new government it would be better to keep out of the university context, where the students were shouting for Africanisation, and even an appointee with his credentials as a fighter of legal battles for blacks against the colonial regime in the past might not escape their ire.

Newspapers sent by friends from over the border gave statistics for the number of what they termed 'refugees' who were entering the neighbouring country. The papers from outside also featured sensationally the inevitable mistakes and misunderstandings, in a new administration, that led to several foreign businessmen being held for investigation by the new regime. For the last fifteen years of colonial rule, Gulf had been drilling for oil in the territory, and just as inevitably it was certain that all sorts of questionable people, from the point of view of the regime's determination not to be exploited preferentially, below the open market for the highest bidder in ideological as well as economic terms, would try to gain concessions.

His wife said, 'The butcher's gone.'

He was home, reading at his desk; he could spend the day more usefully there than at the office, most of the time. She had left after breakfast with her fisherman's basket that she liked to use for shopping, she wasn't away twenty minutes. 'You mean the shop's closed?' There was nothing in the basket. She must have turned and come straight home.

'Gone. It's empty. He's cleared out over the weekend.'

She sat down suddenly on the edge of the desk; and after a moment of silence, both laughed shortly, a strange, secret, complicit laugh. 'Why, do you think?' 'Can't say. He certainly charged, if you wanted a decent cut. But meat's so hard to get, now; I thought it was worth it – justified.'

The lawyer raised his eyebrows and pulled down his mouth: 'Exactly.' They understood; the man probably knew he was marked to run into trouble for profiteering – he must have been paying through the nose for his supplies on the black market, anyway, didn't have much choice.

Shops were being looted by the unemployed and loafers (there had always been a lot of unemployed hanging around for the pickings of the town) who felt the new regime should entitle them to take what they dared not before. Radio and television shops were the most favoured objective for gangs who adopted the freedom fighters' slogans. Transistor radios were the portable luxuries of street life; the new regime issued solemn warnings, over those same radios, that looting and violence would be firmly dealt with but it was difficult for the police to be everywhere at once. Sometimes their actions became street battles, since the struggle with the looters changed character as supporters of the Party's rival political factions joined in with the thieves against the police. It was necessary to be ready to reverse direction, quickly turning down a side street in detour if one encountered such disturbances while driving around town. There were bodies sometimes; both husband and wife had been fortunate enough not to see any close up, so far. A company of the freedom fighters' army was brought down from the north and installed in the barracks to supplement the police force; they patrolled the Quarter, mainly. Muchanga's friend kept his job as gate-keeper although there were armed sentries on guard: the lawyer's wife found that a light touch to mention in letters to relatives in Europe.

'Where'll you go now?'

She slid off the desk and picked up her basket. 'Supermarket, I

37

suppose. Or turn vegetarian.' He knew that she left the room quickly, smiling, because she didn't want him to suggest Muchanga ought to be sent to look for fish in the markets along the wharf in the Quarter. Muchanga was being allowed to indulge in all manner of eccentric refusals; for no reason, unless out of some curious sentiment about her father?

She avoided walking past the barracks because of the machine guns the young sentries had in place of rifles. Rifles pointed into the air but machine guns pointed to the street at the level of different parts of people's bodies, short and tall, the backsides of babies slung on mothers' backs, the round heads of children, her fisherman's basket – she knew she was getting like the others: what she felt was afraid. She wondered what the butcher and his wife had said to each other. Because he was at least one whom she had known. He had sold the meat she had bought that these women and their babies passing her in the street didn't have the money to buy.

It was something quite unexpected and outside their own efforts that decided it. A friend over the border telephoned and offered a place in a lawyers' firm of highest repute there, and some prestige in the world at large, since the team had defended individuals fighting for freedom of the press and militant churchmen upholding freedom of conscience on political issues. A telephone call; as simple as that. The friend said (and the lawyer did not repeat this even to his wife) they would be proud to have a man of his courage and convictions in the firm. He could be satisfied he would be able to uphold the liberal principles everyone knew he had always stood for; there were many whites, in that country still ruled by a white minority, who deplored the injustices under which their black population suffered etc. and believed you couldn't ignore the need for peaceful change etc.

His offices presented no problem; something called Africa

Seabeds (Formosan Chinese who had gained a concession to ship sea-weed and dried shrimps in exchange for rice) took over the lease and the typists. The senior clerks and the current articled clerk (the lawyer had always given a chance to young blacks, long before other people had come round to it – it wasn't only the secretary to the president who owed his start to him) he managed to get employed by the new Trades Union Council; he still knew a few blacks who remembered the times he had acted for black workers in disputes with the colonial government. The house would just have to stand empty, for the time being. It wasn't imposing enough to attract an embassy but maybe it would do for a chargé d'affaires – it was left in the hands of a half-caste letting agent who was likely to stay put: only whites were allowed in, at the country over the border. Getting money out was going to be much more difficult than disposing of the house. The lawyer would have to keep coming back, so long as this remained practicable, hoping to find a loophole in exchange control regulations.

She was deputed to engage the movers. In their innocence, they had thought it as easy as that! Every large vehicle, let alone a pantechnicon, was commandeered for months ahead. She had no choice but to grease a palm, although it went against her principles, it was condoning a practice they believed a young black state must stamp out before corruption took hold. He would take his entire legal library, for a start; that was the most important possession, to him. Neither was particularly attached to furniture. She did not know what there was she felt she really could not do without. Except the plants. And that was out of the question. She could not even mention it. She did not want to leave her towering plants, mostly natives of South America and not Africa, she supposed, whose aerial tubes pushed along the terrace brick, erect tips extending hourly in the growth of the rainy season, whose great leaves turned shields to the spatter of Muchanga's hose glancing off in a shower of harmless arrows, whose two-hand-span trunks were smooth and grooved in one sculptural sweep down their length, or carved by the drop of each dead leaf-stem with concave medallions marking the place and building a pattern at once bold and exquisite. Such things would not travel; they were too big to give away.

The evening she was beginning to pack the books, the telephone rang in the study. Chipande – and he called her by her name, urgently, commandingly – 'What is this all about? Is it true, what I hear? Let me just talk to him – '

'Our friend,' she said, making a long arm, receiver at the end of it, towards her husband.

'But you can't leave!' Chipande shouted down the phone. '*You* can't go! I'm coming round. *Now*.'

She went on packing the legal books while Chipande and her husband were shut up together in the living-room.

'He cried. You know, he actually cried.' Her husband stood in the doorway, alone.

'I know – that's what I've always liked so much about them, whatever they do. They feel.'

The lawyer made a face: there it is, it happened; hard to believe.

'Rushing in here, after nearly a year! I said, but we haven't seen you, all this time . . . he took no notice. Suddenly he starts pressing me to take the university job, raising all sorts of objections, why not this . . . that. And then he really wept, for a moment.'

They got on with packing books like builder and mate deftly handling and catching bricks.

And the morning they were to leave it was all done; twenty-one years of life in that house gone quite easily into one pantechnicon. They were quiet with each other, perhaps out of apprehension of the tedious search of their possessions that would take place at the border; it was said that if you struck over-conscientious or officious freedom fighter patrols they would even make you unload a piano, a refrigerator or washing machine.

She had bought Muchanga a hawker's licence, a hand-cart, and stocks of small commodities. Now that many small shops owned by white shopkeepers had disappeared, there was an opportunity for humble itinerant black traders. Muchanga had lost his fear of the town. He was proud of what she had done for him and she knew he saw himself as a rich merchant; this was the only sort of freedom he understood, after so many years as a servant. But she also knew, and the lawyer sitting beside her in the car knew she knew, that the shortages of the goods Muchanga could sell from his cart, the sugar and soap and matches and pomade and sunglasses, would soon put him out of business. He promised to come back to the house and look after the plants every week; and he stood waving, as he had done every year when they set off on holiday. She did not know what to call out to him as they drove away. The right words would not come again; whatever they were, she left them behind.

# A Hunting Accident

She met her photographer at the Kilimanjaro in Dar. To the new
Missionaries – FAO and UNESCO representatives, Africa-desk
journalists, arts and crafts teachers, Scandinavian documentary
film-makers, Fanonist-Dumontist economist sons and daughters
of dead or departed settler families – this means the hotel, not the
mountain, and the monosyllable stands for Dar es Salaam. She
was dossing down on the floor in the children's bedroom of a
woman professor at the university so she had to wait for an
invitation to his room. She saw at once that the photographer was
not shy but (she hadn't heard of him) was probably somebody, and
not on the look-out for women. It was the old story; she was
accustomed to being taken notice of in a certain way. He sat with
his pipe and old-fashioned oilcloth tobacco pouch in the bar, easy
to find, and put aside his notebooks less to talk than to listen to her
with deep attention; but it was not in that way. He quickly became
her immediate purpose: she didn't show much guile and that was
instinctively wise, because he saw that she had abandoned the
tactics that must serve a pretty girl so well, and she saw that he
would not be able to resist honesty. When she had finished telling
him something in her excited, indignant manner, he would think a
long time, smiling at her, his lips pressed together, small-boned
brown face fine-lined with the growing intensity of his expression,
gazing green eyes darting side-glances away, as if he were
laughing delightedly, privately, within, before he answered with
his 'Why?' 'Would you?' 'I wonder.' He would not have the heart
to reject her.

How exciting it was, to be received on such terms! In the sealed
and carpeted hotel room he opened windows that were never
meant to be opened and the heat-solid night into which she

stretched her arm was even more airless. They agreed that velvet, foam-padded chairs and thick mattresses were Northern luxuries – Southern penances, and she talked of smooth tiles bare to soles, high walls punched free to the sea breeze by lattice. He stroked her sweaty hair away from her cheeks, and it was she who suggested they have a long shower together, he submitting to the old, sweet rites of sensuality with good grace.

It was she who brought him to Ratau's house in another African country. She tried out in her ear how other people might comment: She took him along with her from Tanzania. She thought how she might say to Ratau: Clive Nellen was in Dar, he so much wanted to photograph this country after I'd talked such a lot about it. Both were partly true. She had told him of the country she had been born in, daughter of the colonial Minister of Education, and her standing invitation to come back and stay with the youngest son of her father's old friend, the paramount chief. She had told him of the terracotta and bottle-green town built of red earth with hedges of euphorbia, where the house was, and of the great tree near the house where the tribal court still met each day to decide disputes between citizens. He had come so far, it was a pity not to go farther – perhaps he had been intending to visit that country anyway; he did not discuss plans much. She brought her suitcase and duffle bag of books to his room and slept a last night with him in the hotel before they took an early plane together. They were met at the other end by one of Ratau's big cars with one of his cousins to drive them the hundred-and-twenty kilometres to the chief's town. She watched her photographer's eyes flicking adjustment to the passing scrub and thought how when they were in bed (Ratau would at once understand they should be given a room together) she would be able to say to him: 'Didn't I tell you; that endless plain with a single hill peaked up here and there casting its single blue shadow – it's exactly the imaginary country old maps call "Land of Prester John" or "Kafferland".'

But they got to bed very late and, five or six people, some rather drunk, like noisy innocent children calling to one another from camp bed to sleeping bag, all slept at last before the fire in the living room: Ratau had one of his house-parties. Friends from his university days in England and America, people he invited to stay when he was in various countries at various times, tended to turn up, and there were always also numerous members of the extended family of his father's three wives with a permanent claim on hospitality, taking it for granted that they would serve the household in some way while they were there. Ratau with his cajoling African laugh and his ruthless Cambridge accent had told everyone he was getting them all up to go on a hunting trip in the morning; at half-past six he was prodding at sleepers with his ready-laced boots and holding by the limp hand the little waxen-blonde Swedish potter from the crafts school in the village whom he had taken to the room he, as host, reserved to himself for the night. One of the distant relatives was behind him with a huge tin tray of coffee mugs and rusks. There was something stronger, Ratau called, for those who felt they had to keep out the morning cold. An old kitchen table stocked with brandy and gin and cane spirit stood permanently among the painted barrels of elephant ear and canvas chairs on the huge verandah that hooded the house. The guns were laid out there, too; he was giving orders to relatives summoned to act as bearers, breaking breeches, putting barrels to his left eye. 'Christie – tell me, your friend, what's-his-name? He'll be one of the guns?' And she laughed, a shade disloyally, because Ratau was so attractive, so unselfconsciously male in his natural assumption of what she had been taught, at her progressive school, was the conditioned male role of killer. 'Shoot with his camera,' she said.

'Great. He'll see me get my eland today.'

'Ra-tau! Strictly prohibited! Didn't you tell me eland's protected?'

'A chief's allowed one a year. My brother's turn last time, now I'm going to bag mine.' He lowered his voice, to tease or flirt: *I'll give you the skin to warm you in London.* She murmured, *Mean it?*

*Always mean what I say, Christie.*

The Swedish blonde was not around to hear. When Christine went out onto the gravel drive where a truck had come shaking up under the shouts of some relatives already mounted, she saw her,

44

sitting on a white-washed boulder, yawn like a cat: she was cradling a reluctant toddler with the holy-family reverence Swedish girls display for black children. The photographer was moving about in his unnoticed way among people, his paraphernalia round his neck and bulging the pockets of his usual bush jacket and thin man's large shorts. He gave a hand with lowering the (broken) tail-gate of the truck so that people could climb in but he was not part of the shouting, squealing, laughing and innuendo that made these people who had got to know each other only the previous night feel they were such good friends. He smiled at her as he had before they were lovers; the breasts and thighs and backsides, knees, feet and arms comradely crowded together on the truck seemed to deny the reality of the physical presence he had lent her in a hotel room in Dar. He was certainly married; a passionate boy-and-girl love affair that was the basis of his privacy and whose transformation into domestic peace was the basis of his sympathetic detachment – she would take a bet on it, although she'd never asked him. She hoped, with the edge of defensiveness of one who is at fault, he wasn't sulking because she had said they'd go to the court under the tree and up to the Great Place where the chiefs were buried, this morning. She'd let herself and him be carried off on this hunting party; he might be thinking it was not the kind of thing he would enjoy, but was going along because it was the kind of thing *she* would enjoy – and she couldn't say, explain, excuse anything, lean a seducer's message against his breathing side in the press of the truck, because she was in the cab up front with Ratau driving and a young black woman, Yolisa, while he was in the open truck behind. She turned her head once and could just see him between jolts that brought others into her vision: little Ulla, the Swede, an old relative-retainer in an ancient balaclava, the huge, laughing engineer husband of Yolisa, a great round, neckless head like a Benin bronze bobbing on a vast chest – all with guns poking up between them. No of course her photographer wasn't sulking; he must be at least thirty-eight, not a young man of her own age who talked liberation and expected his girls to do whatever he decided.

Ratau drove with reckless authority through the quiet morning fires of his father's and forefathers' town and forded a river of goats on the road leading out of it. At several points in the open country a figure patched together from whatever the poor in rural areas can assemble against winter cold – scarecrow jackets, split patent shoes, a red knitted cap, a sack serving as a cape, a plaid blanket – rose from a culvert or appeared where cattle had tramped down the grass round a thorn tree. A man came towards the truck as to a rendezvous, hand raised in patient, trusted respect; Ratau landed in an applause of dust, shouting from the window to his bearers on the back, calling to the man on the road, who was, indeed, there by arrangement to report on the movement of game for the information of the hunt. Ratau turned and struck out accordingly across the plain to mopane forest, through mopane forest and out into the open again. In the freedom of driving without a road to follow – a progress as suddenly full of haphazard energy as a speedboat in rough water – the skill and comment and laughter of Ratau, the looming and lurching of gold-red trees, the din of the vehicle's clattering, grinding, chuntering metal bones, the people on the back of the truck seemed not to exist for the three in the cab. Once there was a thump on the roof and Ratau, roaring with laughter, slowed down a bit, but the timing with which he changed back and forth from lower to higher gear and the sureness with which he swung his way through wilderness inspired confidence that in his hands there was no danger to anyone, he would carry everyone through with him, even supposing there actually were to be a load of poor devils somewhere up behind.

In this din and euphoria a gun-shot was hardly more than a pop. It was the ragged scream borne away on the edge of the truck's noise and the battering of fists on the cab roof that made the three in the cab recognise the explosion. Yolisa gave a woman's answering cry to any cry, she clutched Christine's thigh. The truck came to a wild stop, Ratau's smooth black arm extended a hard, efficient barrier to prevent the women pitching to the windscreen. At some second's edge in the collision of seen, heard, felt, Christine saw a large object fall past the truck. She twisted her head to the rear window, feeling her neck snap against its stem; it was Yolisa's husband – not there between the others. His big body flung aside.

46

She imprisoned the black girl's clenched fists in her own; terror sucked her veins flat, she saw herself, them all, standing round this girl's husband, blood running its way, running, running to its ebb and no one with the skill or means to stop it. The helpless struggle of dreams held her in the truck; within that stasis she held fast to the girl to keep death off from her.

And then there was laughter. Shouts: of laughter. The door on the driver's side hung open where Ratau had jumped out. The big engineer was at the window on the passenger's side, signalling his wife to lower it, huffing and puffing, rubbing his right ear, being dusted down by others like a child who has taken a tumble. Christine and the young woman beside her whom she had met twenty-four hours before flung themselves together in a trembling embrace. Like lovers with a moment they cannot share, they hesitated before getting down from the cab. The husband put his arm round his wife as a man does at a party and grinned: 'Don't worry, you're not a widow yet.' She moved her shoulders and looked irritated. Ratau was teasing him, expertly therapeutic against shock. 'Good lord, man, the very sound of a shot and you think you're in the next world.' 'Well, I'm not so sure I'm here now – my ear's burning like hell.' 'Not a scratch to be seen, I assure you. You jumped out of your skin, that's all.' The sun, newly risen ruddy, thrust the gaiety of firelight through bronze, carmine, copper, brown and brass cinders of the dry mopane leaves and the static of goldened dust thrown up around them. The sleep that holds all forests was broken in upon by celebrating voices and unicorn bursts of laughter went bounding away into the solitude. Somebody got down a case of beer from the truck; it was cold as champagne. The cans were passed from mouth to mouth, cala-bash fashion. The gun-bearers in their blue overalls with bare black feet close together against the cold sandy earth, giggled with pleasure. They spoke no English and the little Swedish blonde was taking the opportunity to try and communicate through the few phrases of their language she had already learnt. This one and that gave versions of how the engineer had jumped, toppled, capered, dived from the truck. He slapped at his ear. 'I tell you, quite deaf on that side now. I felt the bullet sear the skin.' Someone crept up and shouted in the ear and he cried out; Ratau stood with commandingly outstretched arm, finger jabbing at him, conducting the general laughter.

She went up almost awkwardly to the photographer; he really did act as if he were incredibly staid! It would give other people the wrong impression of the kind of man she chose. 'You were next to him, weren't you?'

He was lighting the pipe and continued to make small popping noises for a moment or two, those extraordinarily beautiful eyes that had excited her in Dar deeply translucent in three-quarter profile with their expression ellipsed as, at a certain angle, is the design that makes the pupil of a sea-glass marble. He smiled a little at her, round the pipe-stem. 'The bullet went between us – top of my head and his ear.'

Yes – the man she had brought to the party was the smallest and slightest there, when it came to build he didn't look much. 'Good God. What was it like?'

'Loud. He's lucky to be alive. If it'd been an inch to the left, it would have gone over the top of my head, if it'd been an inch to the right, it would've been in his brain.' This was in a low conversational voice no one else would have heard. All he said for the company in general was – more or less to Ratau – as the truck was manned again, 'Perhaps it would be a good idea if everyone checked the guns are unloaded.' Sensible but somehow the kind of dampening suggestion that would come from someone who didn't have quite the style to look danger gallantly in the eye the way this party did. What did he know about the handling of guns, anyway.

Ratau said, not unkindly, 'Don't worry, you'll come to no harm. Everything under control.'

The Swedish girl, already seated in the truck with the defensive smile of a terrified child, held to the hand, cold and tough as the feel of a tortoise's foot, of the old gun-bearer who had never before been touched by a white woman.

Twice the party caught up with three eland who threaded images swiftly into the mopane, a disappearing painted ribbon: the exquisite calligraphy of their broad flanks made them seem two-dimensional. Ratau never got within firing range. If he was disappointed, he was not the kind to show his guests the discourtesy of imposing this upon them; the truck bucked off in other directions, where other game had been reported by the scouts. In a natural park between mopane forests, a herd of red hartebeest grazed. They did not see the threat they did not know. The swaying truck did not fit the shape of any predator. The two women in the cab whispered to each other, 'Look! Look!' at the marvel of a pattern of life printed and yet moving glossy russet and cream, prehistory and yet alive (tails flicked, coats twitched at parasites, droppings fell elegantly); the herd progressed like a cloud or the outline of water, changing without breaking.

Ratau was out of the driver's seat, up onto the open truck. His bearers jumped down lightly knee-bent, spilled all round in a criss-cross of guns. He followed the English protocol; each of his guests must have the chance to drop a beast before he would take a shot himself. The air cracked and split over the truck. The ancient alert was marked by the single majestic signal of a horn-swept head. The herd left the way mercury runs, a mass without distinguishable components. Two hundred yards; and then stopped, the lovely masks facing the hunters. In low gear (beside Christine a relative smelling of clothing impregnated with wood-smoke was driving) the truck followed until within range. The guests fired again at their host's instruction. As a piece of rich cloth is grasped at one end and shaken, a shock-wave passed through the herd. They swung away and this time one could hear the wild hobble of their hooves. Some shapes lay on the ground where they had been; 'Five, we got five!' the engineer shouted. 'Six,' Ratau said, putting a hand on the shoulder of another of his friends. 'You aimed too low, old man; you've got him in the leg. Try for the neck now.' Christine and Yolisa had come down from the cab again. Christine had her hands on her hips, gazing. 'One's standing on its own under that tree, there! Look at that!' 'Albert's wounded him, his hind leg's gone.' 'Oh no!' 'Hop back in, there's a good girl.' She wanted to find the photographer and sit with him on the truck but the men, a herd themselves now, pushed past her unseeingly in their excitement and she had to do as Ratau said and get into the cab.

They rolled slowly across the plain towards the acacia under whose thin gauze of shade the markings of the red hartebeest showed cleanly. All eyes were fixed on it and it took the gaze as if waiting for them. It stood perfectly steady on three legs with the fourth, left hind, dangling snapped at the joint. There was only this disarticulation and a string of bright red blood to break the symmetry of the creature. 'A cow,' someone said; and someone else nodded. Ratau stood for encouragement beside the man whose prey it was. No one shuffled. The shot seemed released from the tension of all, and the beast collapsed, but the cry went up – 'Still alive!' 'My God, finish it off, man!' Ulla and Yolisa covered their ears. 'Ratau, you do it!' But Ratau, the patient host, was instructing: 'Look, like this – you're point-blank, you can't miss – ' Sweating, almost giggling with shame and rage at himself, the guest fired again into his beast that lay there panting, breathing still, looking at him, waiting for the death he owed her. Even that was not a clean shot, though a mortal one. Now she felt herself dying and with the last miracle of co-ordination she could muster drew back her head on the ground and gave a cow's cry, the familiar and gentle, pitiful moo of any clumsy dairy mother. It was as it it were discovered to be true that at midnight on Christmas Eve dumb beasts can speak their sufferings; no one had known that these wild beings could link the abattoir to the hunt, the slave to the free, in that humble bellow. Yolisa and Ulla fled to the cab. Christine stood with the second joint of her forefinger clasped between her bared teeth; she was not thinking of the animal; how horrible this was, he would be thinking, he who had not taken any part, active or vicarious, who had been brought along when what he wanted was to be looking at the Victorian monuments where Ratau's ancestors lay, and watching the council of elders administering the law in the shade of the assembly place, finding sermons in those gravestones and tongues in that tree.

Suddenly she saw he had leapt down from the truck and was walking quickly over to the dying beast. The shorts and veldskoen boots made his small, hard, thin legs look like an ill-nourished schoolboy's, the weighed-down pockets of the bush jacket and the leather straps of two cameras yoked him. He was walking right into the gaze they all decently turned away from. He went straight up to the beast and, down on one knee, began to photograph it again and again, close-up, gazing through the camera, with the camera, into the last moments of life passing in its open eyes. His face was absolutely intent on the techniques he was employing; there was a deep line she had never seen before, drawn down either side of his mouth from the sucked-in nostrils. He placed filters over his lens, removed them. He took his time. The beast tried to open its mouth once more but there was no sound, only a bubble of blood. Its eye (now the head had lolled completely into profile, he could see only one) settled on him almost restfully, the faculty of vision bringing him into focus, then fading, as he himself looked steadily into it with his camera.

He came back to the truck, where Ratau was explaining the reactions of a herd after some of the animals have dropped. She murmured, 'It's still moving' – from afar, the body twitched slackly like a kicked bundle.

'No,' he said. 'She's gone.' He was writing (a date, some figures) in his curling notebook that smelt of tobacco.

The final bag was nineteen – twelve red hartebeest and seven blesbok, most dropped stone-dead with single shots from the host's gun. The eland were not see again. Yolisa sat in the cab, not looking out, and said, 'All I want is to get back and see if my baby's all right.' Another truck arrived, finding its way in the wake of the first as if along signposted city streets, and relatives collected and flung up the carcasses with tremendous admiration and glee, making a party-cloakroom pile of pelts and blood.

The women said they wouldn't touch any of the meat Ratau promised them that night: 'You'll see, red hartebeest is the best eating of any game.' When evening came, and beneath the mantel photograph of the old paramount chief with his looped watch-chain, Homburg hat and leopard skin, the fire spread the delicious incense of burning tambuti wood among the red-wine drinkers, and the hunger of the open air was pleasurable as lust, all ate from the belly-shaped enamel pots a one-eyed relative brought round.

51

'Should have been hung first' – Ratau referred Christine to the English cuisine they both knew – 'But here, with us, nobody wants to wait.' In the kitchen there was feasting, and out in the yard still more people were cooking on a communal open fire. Christine had a lot to drink. She kept an eye on the curiously childlike figure in the old shorts and bush jacket, she was conscious of the smell of his pipe always somewhere in the room, despite the tambuti scent, despite the loudness of the rock music, and she hoped they would get somewhere to sleep alone tonight. She evaded the men who had been dancing with her and found him. 'Are you mad with me?'

He was chatting quietly to an old black man who was trying his tobacco in a home-made pipe. 'Why?'

'Well that's all right then.' She had an urge to kiss passionately that wise-monkey, aesthete's face, to put her hands up under the old khaki clothes and beat her fists at the breast there. He smiled at her affectionately in his appreciation of the old man: she read, 'Go off and enjoy yourself.'

But it was not till the morning that she held his message in her hand. By the time she got up and picked her way among the sleepers on the living-room floor, he had gone with the railway bus that paused, palsied by its sonorous diesel engine, to take on passengers and their small livestock for the capital. He had left a note for her, enclosing another to thank Ratau for his hospitality. Both smelled of proximity to the oilcloth tobacco pouch. 'You'll be glad to know I saw the sun rise from the Great Place today. It's all you said. You've also said there's nowhere else to stay but a Holiday Inn. I'll be based there. For about a week until the 25–6th, I should think. If you should come down, you'll find me queued up at the help-yourself before the curry-and-rice trough, lunchtime.'

She walked through the garden, where butterflies of blossom were alighted on the bauhinia trees and blood-tendoned bones and tufts of hide, dragged from the yard overnight by dogs, littered the oval of ashen winter grass. Flies blundered at her face. Out in the road dust was luxurious as cream underfoot; under the huge tree old men were assembled and a disaffected citizen or two, hat and stick marking formality, awaited the outcome of a long harangue. She hung about, not too near, as if she had only to be able to understand, that's all, and the speaker would have something to say, for her.

# Blinder

Rose lives in the backyard. She has lived there from the time when she washed the napkins of the children in the house, who are now university students. Her husband had disappeared before she took the job. Her lover, Ephraim, who works for Cerberus Security Guards, has lived with her in the yard for as long as anyone in the house can remember. He used to be night watchman at a parking garage, and the children, leaving for school in the morning after Rose had cooked breakfast for them, would meet 'Rose's husband' in his khaki drill uniform, wheeling his bicycle through the gateway as he came off shift. His earlobes were loops that must once have been filled by ornamental plugs, his smile was sweetened by splayed front teeth about which, being what he was, who he was, he was quite unselfconscious.

That is what they remember, the day they hear that he is dead. The news comes by word-of-mouth, as all news seems to in the backyards of the suburb; who is in jail, caught without a pass, and must be bailed out, who has been told to leave a job and backyard at the end of the month, who has heard of the birth of a child, fathered on annual leave, away in the country. There is a howling and keening in the laundry and the lady of the house thinks Rose is off on a blinder again. In her forties Rose began to have what the family and their friends call a drinking problem. Nothing, in the end, has been done about it. The lady of the house thought it might be menopausal, and had Rose examined by her own doctor. He found she had high blood pressure and treated her for that, telling her employer the drinking absolutely must be stopped, it exacerbated hypertension. The lady of the house made enquiries, heard of a Methodist Church that ran a non-racial Alcoholics Anonymous as part of its community programme, and delivered

Rose by car to the weekly meetings in a church hall. Rose calls the AA euphemistically 'my club' and is no longer sloshed and juggling dishes by the family's dinner-hour every night, but she still goes off every two months or so on a week's blinder. There is nothing to be done about it; the lady of the house – the family, the grown children for whom Rose is the innocence of childhood – can't throw her out on the street. She has nowhere to go. If dismissed, what kind of reference can be given her? One can't perjure oneself on the most important of the three requirements of prospective employers: honesty, industry, sobriety.

Over the years, Ephraim has been drawn into discussions about Rose's drinking. Of course, if anyone is able to help her, it should be he, her lover. Though to talk of those two as lovers . . . The men always must have a woman, the women always seem to find a man; if it's not one, then another will do. The lady of the house is the authority who has gone out to the yard from time to time to speak to Ephraim. The man of the house has no time or tact for domestic matters.

Ephraim, what are we going to do about Rose?

I know, madam.

Can't you get her to stop? Can't you see to it that she doesn't keep any of the stuff in the room?

(It is a small room; with two large people living there, Rose and Ephraim, there can't be much space left to hide brandy and beer bottles.)

But she goes round the corner.

(Of course. Shebeens in every lane.)

So what can we do, Ephraim? Can't you talk to her?

What I can do? I talk. Myself, I'm not drinking. The madam ever see me I'm drunk?

I know, Ephraim.

And now Ephraim is dead, they say, and Rose is weeping and gasping in the laundry. The lady of the house does not know whether Rose was in the laundry when one of Ephraim's brothers (as Rose says, meaning his fellow workers) from Cerberus Security Guards came with the news, or whether the laundry, that dank place of greasy slivers of soap, wire coat hangers and cobwebs, was

55

her place to run to, as everyone has a place in which the package of misery is to be unpacked alone, after it is delivered. Rose sits on an upturned bucket and the water from her eyes and nose makes papier mâché heads, in her fist, out of the Floral Bouquet paper handkerchiefs she helps herself to (after such a long service, one can't call it stealing) in the lady of the house's bathroom. Ephraim has been dead a week, although the news comes only now. He went home last week on leave to his village near Umzimkulu. The bus in which he was travelling overturned and he was among those killed. His bicycle, a chain and padlock on the back wheel, is there where he stored it safely against his return, propped beside the washing machine with its murky submarine eye.

It is a delicate matter to know how to deal with Rose. The ordinarily humane thing to do – tell her not to come back into the house to prepare dinner, take off a few days, recover from the shock – is not the humane thing to do, for her. Under that bed of hers on its brick stilts there quickly will be a crate of bottles supplied by willing 'friends'; it is quite natural that someone with her history will turn to drink. So the lady of the house makes a pot of tea and gently calls Rose to their only common ground, the kitchen, and sits with her a while, drinking tea with her on this rare occasion, just as she will go to visit a friend she hasn't seen for years, if he is dying, or will put in a duty appearance at a wedding in some branch of kin from which she has distanced herself in social status, tastes and interests.

Flesh and tears seem to fuse naturally on Rose's face; it is a sight that causes the face itself to be seen afresh, dissolved of so long a familiarity, here in the kitchen, drunk and sober, cooking a leg of lamb as only she can, or grovelling awfully, little plaited horns of dull hair sticking out under the respectability of her maid's cap fallen askew as she so far forgets herself, in embarrassing alcoholic remorse, to try to kiss the hand of the lady of the house. That face – Rose's face – has changed, the lady of the house notices, just as she daily examines the ageing of her own. The fat smooth brown cheeks have resting upon them beneath the eyes two hollowed stains, the colour of a banana skin gone bad. The drinking has stored its poison there, its fatigue and useless repentance. The body is what the sea recently has been discovered to be: an entity into which no abuse can be thrown away, only cast up again.

Rose doesn't ask, what's for dinner? – not tonight. She is scrubbing potatoes, she has taken the T-bone steaks out of the refrigerator, as if this provides a ritual in place of mourning. It is best to leave her to it, the calm of her daily task. The grown children, when they arrive at different intervals later in the afternoon or evening, go one by one back to childhood to put their arms around Rose, this once, again, in the kitchen, and there are tears again from her. They talk about Ephraim, coming home to the backyard early in the morning, just as they were leaving for school, and she actually laughs, a spluttery sob, saying: I used to fry for him some bread and eggs in that fat left from your bacon! – A collusion between the children and the servant over something the lady of the house didn't know, or pretended never to have known. The grown children also recall for Rose how one or other of them, riding a motorcycle or driving a car, passed him only the other day, where he singled himself out, waving and calling a greeting from the uniformed corps in the Cerberus Security Guards transport vehicle. The daughter of the house recently happened to enter the headquarters of a mining corporation, where he was on duty in the glassy foyer with his shabby wolf of a guard dog slumped beside him. She had said, poor thing, put out a hand to stroke it, and Ephraim had expertly jerked the dog away to a safe distance, laughing, while it came to life in a snarl. He's very good with those dogs, Rose says, that dog won't let anyone come near him, *anyone* . . .

But it is over. Ephraim has been buried already; it's all over. She has heard about his death only after he has been buried because she is not the one to be informed officially. He has – had, always had – a wife and children there where he came from, where he was going back to, when he was killed. Oh yes. Rose knows about that. The lady of the house, the family, know about that; it was the usual thing, a young man comes to work in a city, he spends his whole life there away from his home because he has to earn money to send home, and so – the family in the house privately reasoned – his home really is the backyard where his

57

town woman lives? As a socio-political concept the life is a paradigm (the grown child who is studying social science knows) of the break-up of families as a result of the migratory labour system. And that system (the one studying political science knows) ensures that blacks function as units of labour instead of living as men, with the right to bring their families to live in town with them.

But Ephraim deluded himself, apparently, that this backyard where he was so much at home was not his home, and Rose, apparently, accepted his delusion. This was not the first time he had gone home to his wife and children of course. Sometimes the family in the house hadn't noticed his absence at all, until he came back. Rose would be cooking up a strange mess, in the kitchen: Ephraim had brought a chunk of some slaughtered beast for her; she nibbled his gift of sugar-cane, spitting out the fibre. Poor old Rose. No wonder she took to drink (yes, the lady of the house had thought of that, privately) made a convenience of by a man who lived on her and sent his earnings to a wife and children. Now the man dies and Rose is nothing. Nobody. The wife buries him, the wife mourns him. Her children get the bicycle; one of his brothers from Cerberus Security Guards comes to take it from the laundry and bandage it in brown paper and string, foraged from the kitchen, for transport by rail to Umzimkulu.

When the bus flung Ephraim out and he rolled down and died in the brilliant sugar-cane field, he was going home because there was trouble over the land. What land? His father's land, his brothers' land, his land. Rose gives a garbled version anyone from that house, where at least two newspapers a day are read, can interpret: the long-service employee of Cerberus Security Guards was to be spokesman for his family in a dispute over ancestral land granted them by their local chief. Boundary lines have been drawn by government surveyors, on one side there has been a new flag run up, new uniforms put on, speeches made – the portion of the local chief's territory that falls on that side is no longer part of South Africa. The portion that remains on the other side now belongs to the South African government and will be sold to white farmers – Ephraim's father's land, his brothers' land, his land.

58

They are to get some compensation – money, that disappears in school fees and food, not land, that lasts forever.

The lady of the house never does get to hear what happened, now that Ephraim is dead. Rose doesn't say; isn't asked; probably is never told. She appears to get over Ephraim's death very quickly, as these people do, after the first burst of emotion – perhaps it would be better to assume she has to take it philosophically. People whose lives are not easy, poor people, to whom things happen but who don't have the resources to make things happen, don't have the means, either, to extricate themselves from what has happened. Of the remedies of a change of scene, a different job, another man, only the possibility of another man is open to her, and she's no beauty any longer, Rose, even by tolerant black standards. That other remedy – drink – one couldn't say she turns to that, either. Since Ephraim has disappeared from the backyard she drinks neither more nor less. The lady of the house, refurbishing it, thinks of offering an old club armchair to Rose. She asks if there is place in her room, and Rose says, Oh yes! Plenty place.

There is the space that was occupied by Ephraim, his thick spread of legs in khaki drill, his back in braces, his Primus stove and big chromium-fronted radio. Rose spends the whole afternoon cleaning the upholstery with carbon tetrachloride, before getting one of the grown children to help her move the chair across the yard. The lady of the house smiles; there was never any attempt to clean the chair while this was part of the duty of cleaning the house.


On Saturdays, occasionally, all members of the family are home for lunch, as they never are on other days. There is white wine this Saturday, as a treat. Rose has baked a fish dish with a covering of mashed potato corrugated by strokes of a fork and browned crisp along the ridges – it is delicious, the kind of food promoted to luxury class by the everyday norm of cafeterias and fast-food counters. In the middle of the meal, Rose appears in the dining room. The clump of feet that has preceded her gives away that there is someone behind her, out of sight in the passage. The dark hollows under Rose's eyes are wrinkled up with excitement, she shows off: Look who I've got to see you! Look who is here!

The lady of the house is taking good, indulgent, suspicious stock of her, she knows her so well she can tell at once whether or not she's been at the bottle. No – the lady of the house signals with her eyes to the others – Rose is not drunk. Everyone stops eating. Rose is cajoling, high, in her own language, and gesturing back into the passage, her heavy lifted arm showing a shaking jowl of flesh through the tear in her overall – Rose can never be persuaded to mend anything, like the drinking, there is nothing to be done . . . She loses patience – making a quick, conniving face for the eyes of the family – and goes back into the passage to fetch whoever it is. Heads at table return to plates, hands go out for bread or salt. Wine goes to a mouth. Rose shushes and pushes into the room a little group captured and corralled, bringing with them – a draught from another place and time suddenly blowing through the door – odours that have never been in the house before. Hair ruffles along the small dog's back; one of the grown children quickly and secretly puts a hand on its collar. Smell of wood-smoke, of blankets and clothes stored on mud floors between mud walls that live with the seasons, shedding dust and exuding damp that makes things hatch and sprout; smell of condensed milk, of ashes, of rags saved, of wadded newspapers salvaged, of burning paraffin, of thatch, fowl droppings, leaching red soap, of warm skin and fur, cold earth: the family round the table pause over their meal, its flavour and savour are blown away, the utensils they've been eating with remain in their hands, the presence of a strangeness is out of all proportion to the sight of the black country woman and her children, one close beside her, one on her back. The woman never takes her eyes off Rose, who has set her down there. The baby under the blanket closed over her breast with a giant safety-pin cannot be seen except for a green wool bonnet. Only the small child looks round and round the room; the faces, the table, dishes, glasses, flowers, wine bottle; and seems not to breathe. The dog rumbles and its collar is jerked.

Rose is leaning towards the woman, smiling, hands on the sides of her stomach, and encourages her in their language. She displays her to the assembly caught at table. You know who this is, madam? You don't know? She's from Umzimkulu. It's Ephraim's wife. (She swoops up the small child, stiff in her hands.) Ephraim's children. Youngest and second youngest. Look – the baby; it's a little girl. – And she giggles, for the woman who won't respond, can't respond to what is being said about her.

The lady of the house has got up from her chair. She's waiting for Rose to stop jabbering so that she can greet the woman. She goes over to her and puts out her hand, but the woman draws her own palms together and claps them faintly, swaying politely on her feet, which are wearing a pair of men's shoes below thick beaded anklets. So the lady of the house puts a hand on the woman's back, on the blanket that holds the lump of baby, and says to Rose, Tell her I'm very glad to meet her.

As if they were children again, the young people at the table recite the ragged mumble of a greeting, smiling, the males half-rising. The man of the house draws his eyebrows together and nods absently.

She's here about the pension, Rose says, they say she can get a pension from Cerberus Security Guards.

She laughs at the daring, or simpleton trust? – she doesn't know. But the heads around the table know about such things. The children have grown up so clever.

The lady of the house has always been spokesman and diplomat: Did she get anything?

Not yet, they didn't give . . . But they'll write a letter, maybe next month, Rose says, and – this time the performance is surely for the benefit of the country woman instead of the family – leans across to the fruit bowl on a side table and twists off a bunch of grapes which she then pokes at the belly of the small child, who is too immobilised by force of impressions to grasp it. Rose encourages him, coyly, in their langauage, setting him down on his feet.

Rose, says the lady of the house, Give them something to eat, mmh? There's cold meat . . . or if you want to take eggs . . .

Rose says, thank you, mam – procedurally, as if the kitchen were not hers to dispense from, anyway.

The woman has been got in, now there is the manoeuvre of

61

getting her out, she stands as if she would stand for ever, with her baby on her back and her child holding a bunch of grapes that he is afraid to look at, while nobody knows whether to go on eating or wait till Rose takes her away.

The lady of the house is used to making things easy for others: Tell her – thank her for coming to see us.

Rose says something in their language and, after a pause, the woman suddenly begins to speak, turned to Rose but obviously addressing the faces at table through her, through the medium, the mediator of that beer-bloated body, that face ennobled with the bottle's mimesis of the lines and shadings of worldly wisdom. Rose follows with agreeing movements of lips and head, reverberating hum of punctuation. She says: She thanks you. She says goodbye.

Hardly has Rose removed her little troupe when she is back again. Perhaps she remembers the family is eating lunch, has come to ask if they'll want coffee? But no. With exaggerated self-effacement, not looking at anyone else, she asks whether she can talk to the madam a moment?

Now?

Yes, please, now.

The lady of the house follows her into the passage.

Can you borrow me ten rands, please madam?

(This will be an advance on her monthly wages.)

Right away?

Please, mam.

So, interrupting her family meal, the lady of the house goes upstairs and fetches two five rand notes from her purse. She sees Rose, as she comes back down the stairs, waiting in the passage like one of the strangers whose knock at the front door Rose herself will answer but whom she does not let into the living rooms and keeps standing while she goes to call the lady of the house.

Two fives all right? The lady of the house holds out the notes.

Thank you, thanks very much; Rose pushes the money into her overall pocket, that is ripped away at one corner.

For the bus, Rose says, by way of apology for the urgency. Because she's going back there, now, to that place, Umzimkulu.

# A Correspondence Course

Pat Haberman has been alone with Harriet since she divorced Harriet's father. Harriet was five then; too young to be tainted by Haberman's money-grubbing and country-club life – leave that to the children of his second marriage. The maintenance provided for Harriet was always inadequate, but Pat and little Harriet didn't want anything from him, Pat could and did earn their keep, and by the time Harriet was twenty she had her degree and was working on a literacy programme for blacks sponsored by a liberal foundation. Both women do jobs that are more than a way of earning a modest living – Pat (saved, thank god) refers as to a criminal record to the businessmen's dinners, drunken golf-club dances, gymkhanas she left behind with Haberman, and is secretary to the Dean of the Medical School – a fixture there.

Harriet is studying for her Master's by correspondence and has already published a contribution to a symposium on *Literacy and the Media*. She wears German print wrap-around skirts decorated with braid by Xhosa women in a Soweto self-help project, sandals thonged between the toes, and last year cut her shawl of pale brown hair into a permed Afro, so that when she lies soaking in her bath – her mother is amused to see – the hair on her head and her soft pubic hair match.

She is a quiet girl who, her mother is sure, smokes a bit of pot at parties, like all young people today. 'And who are we to talk?' Pat Haberman goes through two packs a day – as she says: just ordinary, lung-destroying tobacco. Once she had a three-year affair with a lawyer who has since left the country, but Harriet was too young at the time to have been aware, and Pat has not decided whether or not to tell her. She is sometimes on the point of doing so: this becomes tempting when she notices that the girl is

63

interested in a new boy. Harriet is probably not as promiscuous as it is customary for her generation to be, but she goes away on paired-off weekend trips and holidays with an often-changing group of friends – the young males leave for military service on the border, or they disappear, fleeing military service. This one or that has skipped; the laconic phrase contains, for all this generation of white South Africans in the know, dumped by their elders with the deadly task of defending a life they haven't chosen for themselves, the singular heritage of their whiteness. Pat and Harriet, mother and daughter, often wonder whether they should not emigrate, too. Harriet has been brought up to realise her life of choices and decent comfort is not shared by the people in whose blackness it is embedded: once protected by them, now threatened. They are all round her; she is not of them. And since she has been adult she has had her place – even if silent – in the ritualistic discussion of what can be done about this by people who have no aptitude for politics but who won't live like Haberman (Harriet, too, thinks of the man who is her father as he was named long ago in the divorce order of Haberman v. Haberman), making money from the blacks and going off to gamble among beauty queens and fellow supermarket kings at the casinos which represent progress in poor, neighbouring black 'states'.

She keeps in touch with her friends who have skipped to Canada or Australia; for a year, now, she has even been writing to a political prisoner at home in South Africa. There his letter was, among circulars from film clubs, bills, and aerogrammes with 'And when are you coming over?' scribbled on the back. *Pretoria Central Prison* – this one rubber-stamped, with the prison censor's signature superimposed. Inside was a closely-handwritten sheet of lined paper neatly torn from an exercise book. *Dear Harriet Haberman*. But her eyes dropped to the signature before reading any further. *Roland Carter*. Slowly skimming the letter as her feet felt their own way down the stone path, she went into the garden where Pat was on her knees among boxes of marigold seedlings.

' "Roland Carter" mean anything to you?'

Her mother's nose was running with the effort of bending and

64

digging; she smeared at it with the back of her earth-caked hand. Harriet repeated: 'Roland – Carter.'

Pat sniffed. 'Of course. He got nine years. The journalist from East London.'

'What did he do? He's written to me . . .'

'Give me my hanky out of my pocket . . . Furthering the aims of the African National Congress, something like that. Smuggled in false identity papers. Or was he one of the pamphlet bomb people? No, that was Cape Town. Can't you remember? – Let's see?'

'Was he the one who said in court he had no regrets?'

'That's him – but what does he write to you about?'

Her mother scrambled up, levering herself from the ground by one firmly-planted palm. The two women stood there in their tiny garden, singled out. 'My god! What a nice letter! Harriet?' She drew back and looked at her daughter, a streak of honest mud on the face of one who recognises the mark of grace on another. They read on. The mother murmured aloud. ' "Your article transported me for more than a whole day . . . I have agreed with you and argued with you . . . some of your conclusions are, forgive me, indefensible . . . so much on my mind that I've decided to take up . . . if you feel you can reply, could you possibly do so next month, as I'm allowed only one letter a month and I'm taking a chance and electing one from you . . ." '

Harriet seemed to read more slowly, or wished to test for herself the business of bringing to life, in her own comprehension, these quotations from Piaget (?) and these shy touches of wit (directed against the writer himself) and sarcasm (directed against the prison warder who would censor the letter). Written in a cell. Sitting on a prison bed. Or did prisoners – white ones, at least – have a table? A window with bars and steel netting (she had seen those, driving past prisons). A heavy door with a warder's spy-hole behind the back bent, writing. 'D'you remember what he looked like?'

Her mother was very confiding. 'Funny enough – I do. You know what a newspaper addict I am. I can see the photograph that was in the papers often during the trial, and then when he was given that ghastly sentence. Nine years . . . A neat, strong – a *sceptical* face. Short nose. A successful face – you know what I mean? He didn't look fanatic. And no beard. Big dark eyes and a brush-cut. More like an athlete . . . one of those pictures of swimmers, after winning a race. Perhaps it was taken when he'd been swimming; a photograph dug up somewhere, probably from his family. I wonder how he managed to get hold of your article? Well, I suppose that sort of academic journal could have been in the prison library. But how did he have our address?'

Harriet showed the envelope, forwarded from the journal.

'Well . . . it's really rather nice to think something you wrote has given a breath of life to someone like this in prison, darling? I told you, you expressed yourself very well – '

The girl smiled. 'I've never even read Piaget.'

Her mother had not touched the letter, only read it over Harriet's shoulder. She held muddy hands away from her sides. 'You're going to write to him?' Piaget was dismissed: 'What does that matter?'

Harriet was waving the letter slowly, as if drying the ink on it. 'I suppose I must.'

'Poor young man. You forget they're in there. Read about the sensation in the papers, and then the years go by.' Pat Haberman looked at her hands, at the plastic boxes of marigolds, her nostrils moving at the rind-bitter, weedy scent of them; she recalled what she had been interrupted at, and got back on her knees.


'How could one refuse?' She flattered the Dean goadingly with this assumption of shared courage of one's convictions. She and the Dean often talk in lowered voices between themselves, although no one can hear them in his inner office where he dictates letters, of the problems of their grown-up children as well as the equally confidential problems of personality clashes among the Medical School staff. There was – no doubt, although she wasn't going to bring it up with Harriet – the likelihood that your name would go into some file. They certainly keep a record of anyone who associates him- or herself in any way with a political prisoner. Even if he wrote to one out of the blue. Even if one had never so much as met him before.

There were often appropriate turns in conversation, among friends or at friends' houses where she met new people, for her to remark on how wonderfully Roland Carter, already four years inside and five to go, kept his spirit unbroken, his mind lively, could still make jokes – her daughter Harriet exchanged letters with him. This remark would immediately 'place' her and her daughter in respect, for people who had not met them before. Sometimes she added what a pity it was that more people who talked liberalism didn't make the effort to write to political prisoners, show them they still were regarded by some as part of the community. Did people realise that in South Africa common criminals, thieves and forgers, were better treated than prisoners of conscience? Roly Carter (after the first few letters he had begun to sign himself simply 'Roly') would get no remission of sentence for good behaviour.

She read Roland Carter's letters – or rather Harriet read them aloud to her – but of course she didn't read those Harriet wrote back. Not that there could be anything particularly personal in them – Harriet had never met the fellow, he was married anyway (Pat had gone to a newspaper library, where a friend of hers worked, and looked up the file of cuttings on his trial), and her letters, like his, would be read by the prison censor. But Harriet was a grown woman, Pat had always respected her child's privacy; in fact taught her, very young, one never ever read anyone else's letters, even if they were left lying about. Harriet typed her letters to Roland Carter in Pretoria Prison; maybe she sensibly wanted to show the prison authorities that all was open to inspection – no ambiguities concealed by illegible handwriting, her law-abiding motive in the correspondence as clear as the type. Pat supposed the letters she heard being composed – Harriet typed slowly, there were long pauses – were much like the letters that came from prison: two young people with shared interests exchanging views on education in Africa. There could be political implications in the subject, heaven knows, but he seemed to assume – and get away with his assumption – that the names of educationalists would belong to too specialised a field for these to be included on the list of Leftist thinkers likely to be familiar to a prison censor.

While the two women were spending a Sunday morning writing their Christmas cards, Pat remarked she supposed prisoners would be allowed to receive cards?

Harriet rarely initiated anything, a stillness in her undisturbed by, quiescently agreeable to her mother's suggestions. 'We can try.'

Christmas; another year of prison, beginning behind those walls. She read through the messages printed on the cards she had bought. *Peace and joy on Christmas Day   Good wishes for the festive season and may the New Year bring every happiness*. She leaned back in her chair.

Her mother was working efficiently: cards, address book, sheets of stamps. 'Are you short? Here, take one of these.'

Harriet wrote, without reading the message, her name below it on a card that showed an otter surfacing amid ripples sold to benefit some wildlife protection society. Pat signed too; Harriet must surely have mentioned in one of the letters that she had a mother?

She remembered to buy Piaget in paperback for what she still thought of as a stocking stuffer, although it was more than ten years since Harriet had been young enough to have a stocking.


Pat Haberman likes to work in the garden for an hour when she comes home from work in the afternoons. When the evening newspaper flops through the slot in the gate onto the grass she looks at the headlines while guiding the jet of the hose with her other hand. She feels at this time of day and in this (she knows) frail set of circumstances – the soothing hiss of the water, the nearness of sunset bird-calls and the distance of the traffic breaking beyond the reef of the quiet suburb – a balance. She ventures out to earn her living every day, but no longer is one of those truly out there, driven by adrenalin and sex hormones, surging along, black skins, white skins, inhaling toxic ambitions, the stresses of solving, of becoming – and what? The five-thirty to six-thirty hour is an illusion of peace in middle age just as the innocence of Cape thrush calls and the freshness of leaves spattered by water from the municipal supply is an illusion of undestroyed nature. Yet while she holds the nozzle of the hose against the snaking energy of piped water's pressure, and reads that a diplomat has been kidnapped, that oil has again been ransomed in the holy money war between the Arabs and the West, even that leaders of the black workers' walk-out at a steel foundry in this same city are being detained by the police, there is this interlude of feeling herself regarding from a base of the calm and eternal what is feverish and constantly whirling away. Later she will read the paper with the background knowledgeability, the watchfulness, the sense of continuity with statements and struggles of black and white, that reasserts involvement and rescues her from that strange pleasant lapse, dangerous white suburban amnesia.

Harriet is out there; she is not deafened by the music in the discothèques, she is not afraid of becoming addicted to drugs. The crack with which the white personality splits and threatens to dribble its endowment like a drying pomegranate is a long way off for her, and perhaps there won't be time enough left for it ever to happen. When she comes home she is on the telephone, or putting in some work on her thesis, or washing her hair preparatory to going out again, in the manner of young girls.

On an evening like any other, the headline Pat saw at once was not the boldest banner; that had to do with a leap in the price of gold. The particular headline was across a double column on the side of the front page; she read it as she picked up in her wet hand the paper from the grass she had just watered. Three long-term political prisoners had escaped from maximum security in Pretoria Prison. The second name was that of Roland Carter. They had all been locked in their cells as usual at 4 p.m. The warder on night patrol had been fooled by dummy bundles placed in their beds. Their disappearance was discovered only at 7 a.m.; it was possible they had a ten- or twelve-hour start on the countrywide search, border post and airport checks now set up to catch them.

Washing her hair: it was over the basin in the bathroom that Pat found Harriet. The girl looked up to her mother's face wide with the sensation of what she had to tell. In a whisper, shoulders hunched: 'He's out.' Pat drew a slithering breath of glee and hugged the paper. 'He's escaped.'

While Harriet read the report her mother was giggling, shaking her clasped hands, unable to keep still. 'Isn't it great? Good for them! Marvellous! It shows you, with enough courage, people never give up.' She speculated over the spitting steak in the pan, between stove and kitchen nook where they ate: 'How many hours to Swaziland? But to the Botswana border, they could be there in five. Supposing they broke out by midnight, they could have been across before the dummies had even been discovered.' Harriet was sent to fetch the AA map out of the glove-box in Pat's car. *Here's to Roly* – Pat clinked her glass against Harriet's, the girl who had kept his spirits up, faithfully written to him for more than a year. The bottle of wine Pat had opened stood next to the map, and various convenient borders were traced from the central point of Pretoria. The men might be on a plane to Europe by now. From Maputo in Mozambique; from Gaborone in Botswana. If they were making for Europe via Zambia, they probably hadn't arrived in Lusaka yet. The radio was clicked on for the news at nine; there was no news: still at large – free. Free!

'What will they do to him if they catch him?'

The girl's question sounded unfair. 'Oh what has he to lose? I suppose some sort of deprivation, solitary confinement. He had nearly four years in there still ahead of him anyway.'

The girl depended on her mother, so well-informed about the strategies of prisoners on the run and their pursuers. 'The police wouldn't shoot them?'

Her mother bunched her mouth, frowning, shaking her head in total reassurance of the absurdity of the idea as she had done when withholding from the child something unpleasant she surely didn't need to know. The thought, *only if they were to resist capture*, was transformed: 'They'd go back where they were, that's all . . .'

Pat appeared at seven in the morning, when the first newscast of the day was broadcast, gliding into her daughter's room with the transistor nursed beside her ear. The curtains were still drawn. Harriet opened her eyes and lay on her back, obedient but not awake. Pat raised her eyebrows high and held up her free hand to stay any distraction when the radio voice referred to the jail-breakers. On the second day a warder was taken into custody on a charge of aiding and abetting. 'Naturally – without help from inside how could they have got out of maximum security? And there must have been brilliant contingency planning – '

'What's that?'

'People outside ready, for weeks or even months, maybe, to act at a given signal exactly as decided upon. Cars, a hideout, money – maybe they've even split up, for safety – '

Harriet slowly came to, out of that deep, helpless morning sleep of the young, who are never tired at night. 'Not his family.'

'No-o! Good lord, no. He wouldn't dare get in touch with *them*.'

'Who?'

'I don't know – associates; it'll be all set up. People they can trust. Maybe from abroad. Somebody could have been brought into the country specially . . .?'

After a week, the three escapers were still at large. At first the radio repeated the same news: that they were believed to be heading for a neighbouring country. Then no mention of them was made at all. The newspapers rephrased the little information the police had released; the authorities in the traditional neighbouring countries of political refuge denied the men had entered their territories. The warder appeared in court, was charged and remanded. There were rumours that one or other of the three had been seen in Gaborone, Lusaka or Maputo. 'Refugee circles' and exiled political organisations in London were 'jubilant' but would make no statement until the men were safely out of Africa. 'One of them's the young man Harriet used to write to, Roland Carter, you know.'

The Dean had heard about that correspondence often enough. 'I shouldn't be too eager to spread that piece of information, if I were you, Pat. The next thing, you'll have the police coming round.'

She tugged smilingly at her ear-ring; at his lily-liveredness.

'They've read all the letters. She's got nothing to hide. They're welcome.'

But the police didn't come; and still the men were not captured. Pat and Harriet Haberman did not know enough about Roland Carter to keep talking of him at every meal they shared. Pat had asked Harriet whether there was ever any kind of inkling, anything at all in the letters that suggested he might . . .? Nothing explicit, of course, but one of those oblique chance remarks one sometimes lets slip, could let slip, even in a letter that was going to be read by a prison censor? But Harriet said there was nothing she could think of; nothing. 'You read the letters, Mum.'

It was so. Yet, pulling up the petunias and marigolds she grew for summer and digging over the earth in preparation for daffodils and freesias, she heard or mouthed phrases from the letters. People of the same generation understand things differently from the way they are understood by one of another generation. Turns of phrase. Vocabulary – words change meanings (take the adjective 'gay' . . .). The phrases presented themselves to her from somewhere. As she dug and then forked and raked, hearing a sizzling in her ears, closer than the bird-calls, from the dizzying effort, sometimes she had the feeling that *he* was thinking of her rather than she of him – although he didn't know her, it was not to her he had written. She most likely never had been mentioned; if he had not been allowed to receive the Christmas card that time, he might not know she existed. Somewhere: out there in the distant traffic, the traffic of the world, their prisoner – hers and Harriet's – *he* existed as another being who was no longer a prisoner. He suffered, perhaps. He hid. He was hungry; and hunted. Literally: they used dogs with faithful names like *Wagter, †Boetie, who attacked on command. He prowled in those swamps of the cities, the Hillbrow bars where everybody was immigrant and an unrecognised stranger, the drinking places of blacks in urine-smelling lanes where nameless whites could buy pot, or he yanked again and again at the handle of a fruit machine, bullying luck, one among the crowds in their uniform of humorous

*Watchman    †Brother

72

T-shirts in a casino across the border, his danger ticking for him, a parcel-bomb left in a gold plastic bag of exactly the type their women carried. The grip on the commonplace and eternal she took with this earth that she handled, lost its meaning. It was only dirt her hands were coated in as a black servant's hands are coated with white gloves when he waits at table in certain pretentious houses (Haberman's). Somewhere out there beyond her garden a suburban burglar alarm went Wagnerian and there was the flying wail of ambulances and police cars. The bulbs she had saved from last year were going to be buried in this cloying, suffocating earth and would live again; but when a human being is at last shut in it she will never break out.

She had begun to check the doors and windows before switching off her bedroom light at night. She held breath, moving in Harriet's room, but the girl did not ever know she was there. She bolted the gate, which they never bothered to do, and since she was sure to be awake first in the mornings, could unbolt it again before her daughter got up. Once Harriet complained her room was stuffy; she had found her window shut. Yes, her mother thought she'd heard something – that old tom cat who used to jump in and had once pissed against Harriet's dressing-gown – so she had got up in the night to close it. They laughed a little at the reminder of the dreadful cat.

'With the window shut, the smell still comes back.'

'I'm sorry, darling. I'll shampoo that bit of carpet again.'

If Harriet noticed that all doors and windows were locked now, she said nothing. One early morning when Pat went across the lawn in pyjamas to slide back the bolt the morning paper was not on the grass – must have fallen backwards through the slot. She opened the gate. The paper was there outside, on the pavement; as she bent for it her eyes were on a level with a bundle that had been left half-concealed (if you were to have been upright, chances were you would have missed it) by the jasmine that incorporated in its thicket an old wire fence between the garden and a lane that divided their cottage from the next property. Placed, not left. The unisex clothing in a tramp's bundle was Harriet's jeans, the too-big pair she hardly wore, the Mykonos fisherman's sweater from

73

her trip, the men's thick socks young girls had a fad to wear with clogs. In just this way she had put out milk for the fairies (or stray cats?) when she was a little girl. She had believed in the Easter bunny when on Easter morning she found chocolate eggs hidden like this . . . The paper Pat held carried a report from reliable sources that the Russians had planned and executed the prison-break and the three political prisoners were believed to be already in Moscow.

Whether Harriet had taken the offering back in again herself, or whether one of the white tramps or black out-of-works who frequented the lane had had a windfall, the bundle was not there two days later. Pat said nothing. Just as long ago, she didn't want to make the child feel foolish.


On the evening a man appeared at the open kitchen door. Harriet did not know who it was but Pat Haberman recognised him instantly. Hiccups of fear loosed inside her. They were uncontroll-able but her body stood there and barred what was beyond the limit, more than could be expected or asked. He saw she knew him; drew down a smile in acknowledgement of the claim he represented, and said, You are alone?

And at that, Harriet stood up calmly as if she had heard her named called; and went to close the door behind him.

Liquid flashes like the sweeps of heat that had gone through her blood at fifty took Pat to her bedroom. She locked that door, wanted to beat upon it, whimper. She went and sat on her bed, hands clamped together between her thighs. The walls that closed her in were observing her. She tried not to hear the voices that came through them; even a subdued laugh. She stood up and paced out the room with the hesitancy of anguish. To do something with her hands she filled a tooth-glass at the washhand basin and, a prisoner tending his one sprig of green, gave water to the pot of African violets for what she had done, done to her darling girl, *done for*.

# The Termitary

When you live in a small town far from the world you read about in municipal library books, the advent of repair men in the house is a festival. Daily life is gaily broken open, improvisation takes over. The living-room masquerades as a bedroom while the smell of paint in the bedroom makes it uninhabitable. The secret backs of confident objects (matchwood draped with cobwebs thickened by dust) are given away when furniture is piled to the centre of the room. Meals are picnics at which table manners are suspended because the first principle of deportment drummed into children by their mother – sitting down at table – is missing: there is nowhere to sit. People are excused eccentricities of dress because no one can find anything in its place.

A doctor is also a kind of repair man. When he is expected the sheets are changed and the dog chased off the patient's bed. If a child is sick, she doesn't have to go to school, she is on holiday, with presents into the bargain – a whole roll of comics tied with newsagent's string, and crayons or card games. The mother is alone in the house, except for the patient out of earshot in the sickroom; the other children are at school. Her husband is away at work. She takes off her apron, combs her hair and puts on a bit of lipstick to make herself decent for the doctor, setting ready a tea-tray for two in the quiet privacy of the deserted living-room as for a secret morning visit from the lover she does not have. After she and the doctor, who smells intoxicating, coldly sweet because he has just come from the operating theatre, have stood together looking down at the patient and making jolly remarks, he is glad to accept a cup of tea in his busy morning round and their voices are a murmur and an occasional rise of laughter from behind the closed living-room door.

75

Plumber, painter, doctor; with their arrival something has happened where nothing ever happens; at home: a house with a bungalow face made of two bow-window eyes on either side of a front-door mouth, in a street in a gold-mining town of twenty-five thousand people in South Africa in the 1930s.

Once the upright Steinway piano stood alone on the few remaining boards of a room from which the floor had been ripped. I burst in to look at the time on the chiming clock that should have been standing on the mantelpiece and instead flew through the air and found myself jolted down into a subterranean smell of an earth I'd never smelt before, the earth buried by our house. I was nine years old and the drop broke no bones; the shock excited me, the thought of that hollow, earth-breaking dark always beneath our Axminster thrilled me; the importance I gained in my mother's accounts of how I might so easily have injured myself added to the sense of occasion usual in the family when there were workmen in.

This time it was not the painters, Mr Strydom and his boys, over whom my mother raised a quarrel every few years. *I'm not like any other woman. I haven't got a husband like other women's. The state this house is in. You'd see the place fall to pieces before you'd lift a finger. Too mean to pay for a lick of paint, and then when you do you expect it to last ten years. I haven't got a home like other women.* Workmen were treated as the house-guests we never had; my mother's friends were neighbours, my father had none, and she wouldn't give house-room to a spare bed, anyway, because she didn't want his relatives coming. Mr Strydom was served sweet strong tea to his taste many times a day, while my mother stood by to chat and I followed his skills with the brush, particularly fascinated when he was doing something he called, in his Afrikaner's English, 'pulling the line'. This was the free-hand deftness with which he could make a narrow black stripe dividing the lower half of our passage, painted dark against dirty fingerprints, from the cream upper half. *Yust a sec while I first pull the line, ay.*

Then he would drain his cup so completely that the tea leaves swirled up and stuck to the sides. This workmanlike thirst, for me, was a foreign custom, sign of the difference between being

Afrikaans and English, as we were, just as I accepted that it must be in accordance with *their* custom that the black 'boys' drank their tea from jam tins in the yard. But Mr Strydom, like the doctor, like deaf dapper Mr Waite the electrician, who had drinking bouts because he had been through something called Ypres, and Mr Hartman who sang to himself in a sad soprano while he tuned the Steinway upright my mother had brought from her own mother's house, was a recurrent event. The state the house was in, this time, was one without precedent; the men who were in were not repair men. They had been sent for to exterminate what we called white ants – termites who were eating our house away under our feet. A million jaws were devouring steadily night and day the timber that supported our unchanging routines: one day (if my mother hadn't done something about it you may be sure no one else would) that heavy Steinway in its real rosewood case would have crashed through the floor-boards.

For years my mother had efficiently kicked apart the finely-granulated earth, forming cones perfect as the shape taken by sand that has trickled through an egg-timer, that was piled in our garden by ordinary black ants. My father never did a hand's turn; she herself poured a tar-smelling disinfectant down the ant-holes and emptied into them kettles of boiling water that made the ground break out in a sweat of gleaming, struggling, pin-head creatures in paroxysm. Yet (it was another event) on certain summer evenings after rain we would rush out into the garden to be in the tropical snowfall of millions of transparent wings from what we called flying ants, who appeared from nowhere. We watched while frogs bold with greed hopped onto the verandah to fill their pouched throats with these apparently harmless insects, and our cat ate steadily but with more self-control, spitting out with a shake of her whiskers any fragment of wing she might have taken up by mistake. We did not know that when these creatures shed their four delicate dragon-fly wings (some seemed to struggle like people getting out of coats) and became drab terrestrials, and some idiotically lifted their hindquarters in the air as if they were reacting to injury, they were enacting a nuptial ceremony that, one summer night or another, had ended in one out of these millions being fertilised and making her way under our house to become queen of a whole colony generated and given birth to by herself. Somewhere under our house she was in an endless parturition that would go on until she was found and killed.

The men had been sent for to search out the queen. No evil-smelling poisons, no opening-up of the tunnels more skilfully constructed than the London Underground, the Paris Metro or the New York subway I'd read about, no fumigation such as might do for cockroaches or moles or wood-borer beetles, could eradicate termites. No matter how many thousands were killed by my mother, as, in the course of the excavations that tore up the floor-boards of her house, the brittle passages made of grains of earth cemented by a secretion carried in the termites' own bodies were broken, and the inhabitants poured out in a pus of white moving droplets with yellow heads – no matter how many she cast into death agony with her Flit spray, the termitary would at once be repopulated so long as the queen remained, alive, hidden in that inner chamber where her subjects who were also her progeny had walled her in and guarded and tended her.

The three exterminators were one white and two black. All had the red earth of underground clinging to their clothes and skin and hair; their eyes were bloodshot; the nails of their hands, black or white, were outlined in red, their ears rimmed. The long hairs in the nostrils of the white man were coated with red as a bee's legs are yellow with pollen. These men themselves appeared to have been dug up, raw from that clinging earth entombed beneath buildings. Bloodied by their life-long medieval quest, they were ready to take it up once more: the search for a queen. They were said to be very good; my mother was sceptical as she was about the powers of water-diviners with bent twigs or people who got the dead to spell out messages by moving a glass to letters of the alphabet. But what else could she do? My father left it all to her, she had the responsibility.

She didn't like the look of these men. They were so filthy with earth; hands like exposed roots reaching for the tea she brought. She served even the white man with a tin mug.

It was she who insisted they leave a few boards intact under the

78

piano; she knew better than to trust them to move it without damage to the rosewood case. They didn't speak while children watched them at work. The only sound was the pick stopped by the density of the earth under our living-room, and the gasp of the black man who wielded the pick, pulling it free and hurling it back into the earth again. Held off by silence, we children would not go away. We stolidly spent all our free time in witness. Yet in spite of our vigilance, when it happened, when they found her, at last – the queen – we were not there.

My mother was mixing a cake and we had been attracted away to her by that substance of her alchemy that was not the beaten eggs and butter and sugar that went into it; even the lightest stroke of a quick forefinger into the bowl conveyed a coating of fragrant creamy sweetness to the mouth which already had foreknowledge of its utter satisfaction through the scent of vanilla that came not only from the bowl, but from her clothes, her hair, her very skin. Suddenly my mother's dog lifted his twitching lip back over his long teeth and began to bounce towards and back away from the screen door as he did when any stranger approached her. We looked up; the three men had come to the back steps. The white gestured his ochre hand brusquely at one of the blacks, who tramped forward with a child's cardboard shoe-box offered. The lid was on and there were rough air-holes punched in it here and there, just as in the boxes where we had kept silk worms until my mother thought they smelled too musty and threw them away. The white man gestured again; he and my mother for a moment held their hands the same way, his covered with earth, hers with flour. The black man took off the lid.

And there she was, the queen. The smallest child swallowed as if about to retch and ran away to the far side of the kitchen. The rest of us crowded nearer, but my mother made us make way, she wasn't going to be fobbed off with anything but complete satisfaction for her husband's money. We all gazed at an obese, helpless white creature, five inches long, with the tiny, shiny-visored head of an ant at one end. The body was a sort of dropsical sac attached to this head; it had no legs that could be seen, neither could it propel itself by peristaltic action, like a slug or worm. The

79

queen. The queen whose domain, we had seen for ourselves in the galleries and passages that had been uncovered beneath our house, was as big as ours.

The white man spoke. 'That's 'er, missus.'

'You're sure you've got the queen?'

'We got it. That's it.' He gave a professional snigger at ignorance.

Was she alive? – But again the silence of the red-eyed, red-earthed men kept us back; they wouldn't let us daringly put out a finger to touch that body that seemed blown up in sections, like certain party balloons, and that had at once the suggestion of tactile attraction and repugnance – if a finger were to be stroked testingly along that perhaps faintly downy body, sweet and creamy stuff might be expected to ooze from it. And in fact, when I found a book in the library called *The Soul of the White Ant*, by Eugène Marais, an Afrikaner like the white man who had found the queen's secret chamber, I read that the children-subjects at certain times draw nourishment from a queen's great body by stroking it so that she exudes her own rich maternal elixir.

'Ughh. Why's she so fat?' The smallest child had come close enough to force himself to look again.

'S'es full of ecks,' the white man said. 'They lays about a million ecks a day.'

'Is it dead?'

But the man only laughed, now that his job was done, and like the showman's helper at the conclusion of an act, the black man knew to clap the lid back on the shoe-box. There was no way for us to tell; the queen cannot move, she is blind; whether she is underground, the tyrannical prisoner of her subjects who would not have been born and cannot live without her, or whether she is captured and borne away in a shoe-box, she is helpless to evade the consequences of her power.

My mother paid the men out of her housekeeping allowance (but she would have to speak to our father about that) and they nailed back the living-room floor-boards and went away, taking the cardboard box with them. My mother had heard that the whole thing was a hoax; these men went from house to house, made the terrible mess they'd left hers in, and produced the same queen time and again, carrying it around with them.

Yet the termites left our house. We never had to have those particular workmen in again. The Axminster carpet was laid once more, the furniture put back in its place, and I had to do the daily half-hour practice on the Steinway that I had been freed of for a week. I read in the book from the library that when the queen dies or is taken away all the termites leave their posts and desert the termitary; some find their way to other communities, thousands die. The termitary with its fungus-gardens for food, its tunnels for conveying water from as much as forty feet underground, its elaborate defence and communications system, is abandoned.

We lived on, above the ruin. The children grew up and left the town; coming back from the war after 1946 and later from visits to Europe and America and the Far East, it bored them to hear the same old stories, to be asked: 'D'you remember Mr Hartman who used to come in to tune the piano? He was asking after you the other day – poor thing, he's crippled with arthritis.' 'D'you remember old Strydom, "pulling the line" . . . how you kids used to laugh, I was quite ashamed . . .' 'D'you remember the time the white ant men were in, and you nearly broke your leg?' Were these events the sum of my mother's life? Why should I remember? I, who – shuddering to look back at those five rooms behind the bow-window eyes and the front-door mouth – have oceans, continents, snowed-in capitals, islands where turtles swim, cathedrals, theatres, palace gardens where people kiss and tramps drink wine – all these to remember. My father grew senile and she put him in a home for his last years. She stayed on, although she said she didn't want to; the house was a burden to her, she had carried the whole responsibility for him, for all of us, all her life. Now she is dead and although I suppose someone else lives in her house, the secret passages, the inner chamber in which she was our queen and our prisoner are sealed up, empty.

# Crimes of Conscience

Apparently they noticed each other at the same moment, coming down the steps of the Supreme Court on the third day of the trial. By then casual spectators who come for a look at the accused – to see for themselves who will risk prison walls round their bodies for ideas in their heads – have satisfied curiosity; only those who have some special interest attend day after day. He could have been a journalist; or an aide to the representative of one of the Western powers who 'observe' political trials in countries problematic for foreign policy and subject to human rights lobbying back in Western Europe and America. He wore a corduroy suit of unfamiliar cut. But when he spoke it was clear he was, like her, someone at home – he had the accent, and the casual, colloquial turn of phrase. 'What a session! I don't know . . . After two hours of that . . . feel like I'm caught in a roll of sticky tape . . . unreal . . .'

There was no mistaking her. She was a young woman whose cultivated gentleness of expression and shabby homespun style of dress, in the context in which she was encountered, suggested not transcendental meditation centre or environmental concern group or design studio, but a sign of identification with the humanity of those who had nothing and risked themselves. Her only adornment, a necklace of minute ostrich-shell discs stacked along a thread, moved tight at the base of her throat tendons as she smiled and agreed. 'Lawyers work like that . . . I've noticed. The first few days, it's a matter of people trying each to confuse the other side.'

Later in the week, they had coffee together during the court's lunch adjournment. He expressed some naïve impressions of the trial, but as if fully aware of gullibility. Why did the State call witnesses who came right out and said the regime oppressed their spirits and frustrated their normal ambitions? Surely that kind of testimony favoured the defence, when the issue was a crime of conscience? She shook fine hair, ripply as a mohair rug. 'Just wait. Just wait. That's to establish credibility. To prove their involvement with the accused, their intimate knowledge of what the accused said and did, to *inculpate* the accused in what the defence's going to deny. Don't you see?'

'Now I see.' He smiled at himself. 'When I was here before, I didn't take much interest in political things . . . activist politics, I suppose you'd call it? It's only since I've been back from overseas . . .'

She asked conversationally what was expected of her: how long had he been away?

'Nearly five years. Advertising, then computers . . .' The dying-out of the sentence suggested the lack of interest in which these careers had petered. 'Two years ago I just felt I wanted to come back. I couldn't give myself a real reason. I've been doing the same sort of work here – actually, I ran a course at the business school of a university, this year – and I'm slowly beginning to find out *why* I wanted to. To come back. It seems it's something to do with things like *this*.'

She had a face that showed her mind following another's; eyebrows and mouth expressed quiet understanding.

'I imagine all this sounds rather feeble to you. I don't suppose you're someone who stands on the sidelines.'

Her thin, knobbly little hands were like tools laid upon the formica counter of the coffee bar. In a moment of absence from their capability, they fiddled with the sugar sachets while she answered. 'What makes you think that?'

'You seem to know so much. As if you'd been through it yourself . . . Or maybe . . . you're a law student?'

'Me? Good lord, no.' After one or two swallows of coffee, she offered a friendly response. 'I work for a correspondence college.'

'Teacher.'

Smiling again: 'Teaching people I never see.'

'That doesn't fit too well. You look the kind of person who's more involved.'

For the first time, polite interest changed, warmed. 'That's what you missed, in London? Not being involved . . .?'

At that meeting he gave her a name, and she told him hers.


The name was Derek Felterman. It was his real name. He *had* spent five years in London; he *had* worked in an advertising company and then studied computer science at an appropriate institution, and it was in London that he was recruited by someone from the Embassy who wasn't a diplomat but a representative of the internal security section of State security in his native country. Nobody knows how secret police recognise likely candidates; it is as mysterious as sexing chickens. But if the definitive characteristic sought is there to be recognised, the recruiting agent will see it, no matter how deeply the individual may hide his likely candidacy from himself.

He was not employed to infiltrate refugee circles plotting abroad. It was decided that he would come home 'clean', and begin work in the political backwater of a coastal town, on a university campus. Then he was sent north to the mining and industrial centre of the country, told to get himself an ordinary commercial job without campus connections, and, as a new face, seek contacts wherever the information his employers wanted was likely to be let slip – left-wing cultural gatherings, poster-waving protest groups, the public gallery at political trials. His employers trusted him to know how to ingratiate himself; that was one of the qualities he had been fancied for, as a woman might fancy him for some other characteristic over which he had no volition – the way one corner of his mouth curled when he smiled, or the brown gloss of his eyes.

He, in his turn, had quickly recognised her – first as a type, and then, the third day, when he went away from the court for verification of her in police files, as the girl who had gone secretly to visit a woman friend who was under House Arrest, and subsequently had served a three-month jail sentence for refusing to testify in a case brought against the woman for breaking her isolation ban. Aly, she had called herself. Alison Jane Ross. There was no direct connection to be found between Alison Jane Ross's interest in the present trial and the individuals on trial; but from the point of view of his avocation this did not exclude her possible involvement with a master organisation or back-up group involved in continuing action of the subversive kind the charges named.

Felterman literally moved in to friendship with her, carrying a heavy case of books and a portable grill. He had asked if she would come to see a play with him on Saturday night. Alas, she was moving house that Saturday; perhaps he'd like to come and help, instead? The suggestion was added, tongue-in-cheek at her own presumption. He was there on time. Her family of friends, introduced by diminutives of their names, provided a combined service of old combi, springless station-wagon, take-away food and affectionate energy to fuel and accomplish the move from a flat to a tiny house with an ancient palm tree filling a square of garden, grating its dried fronds in the wind with the sound of a giant insect rubbing its legs together. To the night-song of that creature they made love for the first time a month later. Although all the Robs, Jimbos and Ricks, as well as the Jojos, Bets and Lils, kissed and hugged their friend Aly, there seemed to be no lover about who had therefore been supplanted. On the particular, delicate path of intimacy along which she drew him or that he laid out before her, there was room only for the two of them. At the beginning of ease between them, even before they were lovers, she had come of herself to the stage of mentioning that experience of going to prison, but she talked of it always in banal surface terms – how the blankets smelled of disinfectant and the chief wardress's cat used to do the inspection round with its mistress. Now she did not ask him about other women, although he was moved, occasionally, in some involuntary warm welling-up complementary to that other tide – of sexual pleasure spent – to confess by the indirection of an anecdote, past affairs, women who had had their time and place. When the right moment came naturally to her, she told without shame, resentment or vanity that she had just spent a year 'on her own' as something she felt she needed after living for three years with someone who, in the end, went back to his wife. Lately there had been one or two brief affairs – 'Sometimes – don't you find – an

85

old friend suddenly becomes something else . . . just for a little while, as if a face is turned to another angle . . .? And next day, it's the same old one again. Nothing's changed.'

'Friends are the most important thing for you, aren't they? I mean, everybody has friends, but you . . . You'd really do *anything*. For your friends. Wouldn't you?'

There seemed to come from her reaction rather than his words a reference to the three months she had spent in prison. She lifted the curly pelmet of hair from her forehead and the freckles faded against a flush colouring beneath: 'And they for me.'

'It's not just a matter of friendship, either – of course, I see that. Comrades – a band of brothers . . .'

She saw him as a child staring through a window at others playing. She leant over and took up his hand, kissed him with the kind of caress they had not exchanged before, on each eyelid.

Nevertheless her friends were a little neglected in favour of him. He would have liked to have been taken into the group more closely, but it is normal for two people involved in a passionate love affair to draw apart from others for a while. It would have looked unnatural to press to behave otherwise. It was also understood between them that Felterman didn't have much more than acquaintances to neglect; five years abroad and then two in the coastal town accounted for that. He revived for her pleasures she had left behind as a schoolgirl: took her water-skiing and climbing. They went to see indigenous people's theatre together, part of a course in the politics of culture she was giving him not by correspondence, without being aware of what she was doing and without giving it any such pompous name. She was not to be persuaded to go to a discothèque, but one of the valuable contacts he did have with her group of friends of different races and colours was an assumption that he would be with her at their parties, where she out-danced him, having been taught by blacks how to use her body to music. She was wild and nearly lovely, in this transformation, from where he drank and watched her and her associates at play. Every now and then she would come back to him: an offering, along with the food and drink she carried. As months went by, he was beginning to distinguish certain patterns

86

in her friendships; these were extended beyond his life with her into proscribed places and among people restricted by law from contact, like the woman for whom she had gone to prison. Slowly she gained the confidence to introduce him to risk, never discussing but evidently always sensitively trying to guage how much he really wanted to find out if 'why he wanted to come back' had to do with 'things like this'.

It was more and more difficult to leave her, even for one night, going out late, alone under the dry, chill agitation of the old palm tree, rustling through its files. But although he knew his place had been made for him to live in the cottage with her, he had to go back to his flat that was hardly more than an office, now, unoccupied except for the chair and dusty table at which he sat down to write his reports: he could hardly write them in the house he shared with her.

She spoke often of her time in prison. She herself was the one to find openings for the subject. But even now, when they lay in one another's arms, out of reach, undiscoverable to any investigation, out of scrutiny, she did not seem able to tell of the experience what there really was in her being, necessary to be told: why she risked, for whom and what she was committed. She seemed to be waiting passionately to be given the words, the key. From him.

It was a password he did not have. It was a code that was not supplied him.

And then one night it came to him; he found a code of his own; that night he had to speak. 'I've been spying on you.'

Her face drew into a moment of concentration akin to the animal world, where a threatened creature can turn into a ball of spikes or take on a fearsome aspect of blown-up muscle and defensive garishness.

The moment left her face instantly as it had taken her. He had turned away before it as a man does with a gun in his back.

She shuffled across the bed on her haunches and took his head in her hands, holding him.

# Oral History

There's always been one house like a white man's house in the village of Dilolo. Built of brick with a roof that bounced signals from the sun. You could see it through the mopane trees as you did the flash of paraffin tins the women carried on their heads, bringing water from the river. The rest of the village was built of river mud, grey, shaped by the hollows of hands, with reed thatch and poles of mopane from which the leaves had been ripped like fish-scales.

It was the chief's house. Some chiefs have a car as well but this was not an important chief, the clan is too small for that, and he had the usual stipend from the government. If they had given him a car he would have had no use for it. There is no road: the army patrol Land Rovers come upon the people's cattle, startled as buck, in the mopane scrub. The village has been there a long time. The chief's grandfather was the clan's grandfathers' chief, and his name is the same as that of the chief who waved his warriors to down assegais and took the first Bible from a Scottish Mission Board white man. *Seek and ye shall find*, the missionaries said.

The villagers in those parts don't look up, any more, when the sting-shaped army planes fly over twice a day. Only fish-eagles are disturbed, take off, screaming, keen swerving heads lifting into their invaded domain of sky. The men who have been away to work on the mines can read, but there are no newspapers. The people hear over the radio the government's count of how many army trucks have been blown up, how many white soldiers are going to be buried with *full military honours* – something that is apparently white people's way with their dead.

The chief had a radio, and he could read. He read to the headmen the letter from the government saying that anyone hiding or giving food and water to those who were fighting against the government's army would be put in prison. He read another letter from the government saying that to protect the village from these men who went over the border and came back with guns to kill people and burn huts, anybody who walked in the bush after dark would be shot. Some of the young men who, going courting or drinking to the next village, might have been in danger, were no longer at home in their fathers' care anyway. The young go away: once it was to the mines, now – the radio said – it was over the border to learn how to fight. Sons walked out of the clearing of mud huts; past the chief's house; past the children playing with the models of police patrol Land Rovers made out of twisted wire. The children called out, Where are you going? The young men didn't answer and they hadn't come back.

There was a church of mopane and mud with a mopane flagpole to fly a white flag when somebody died; the funeral service was more or less the same Protestant one the missionaries brought from Scotland and it was combined with older rituals to entrust the newly-dead to the ancestors. Ululating women with whitened faces sent them on their way to the missionaries' last judgment. The children were baptised with names chosen by portent in consultation between the mother and an old man who read immutable fate in the fall of small bones cast like dice from a horn cup. On all occasions and most Saturday nights there was a beer-drink, which the chief attended. An upright chair from his house was brought out for him although everyone else squatted comfortably on the sand, and he was offered the first taste from an old decorated gourd dipper (other people drank from baked-bean or pilchard tins) – it is the way of people of the village.

It is also the way of the tribe to which the clan belongs and the subcontinent to which the tribe belongs, from Matadi in the west to Mombasa in the east, from Entebbe in the north to Empangeni in the south, that everyone is welcome at a beer-drink. No traveller or passer-by, poling down the river in his pirogue, leaving the snake-skin trail of his bicycle wheels through the sand, betraying his approach – if the dogs are sleeping by the cooking fires and the children have left their home-made highways – only by the brittle fragmentation of the dead leaves as he comes unseen through miles of mopane, is a presence to be questioned. Everyone for a long way round on both sides of the border near Dilolo has a black skin, speaks the same language and shares the custom of hospitality. Before the government started to shoot people at night to stop more young men leaving when no one was awake to ask, 'Where are you going?' people thought nothing of walking ten miles from one village to another for a beer-drink.

But unfamiliar faces have become unusual. If the firelight caught such a face, it backed into darkness. No one remarked the face. Not even the smallest child who never took its eyes off it, crouching down among the knees of men with soft, little boy's lips held in wonderingly over teeth as if an invisible grown-up hand were clamped there. The young girls giggled and flirted from the background, as usual. The older men didn't ask for news of relatives or friends outside the village. The chief seemed not to see one face or faces in distinction from any other. His eyes came to rest instead on some of the older men. He gazed and they felt it.

Coming out of the back door of his brick house with its polished concrete steps, early in the morning, he hailed one of them. The man was passing with his hobbling cows and steadily bleating goats; stopped, with the turn of one who will continue on his way in a moment almost without breaking step. But the summons was for him. The chief wore a frayed collarless shirt and old trousers, like the man, but he was never barefoot. In the hand with a big steel watch on the wrist, he carried his thick-framed spectacles, and drew down his nose between the fingers of the other hand; he had the authoritative body of a man who still has his sexual powers but his eyes flickered against the light of the sun and secreted flecks of matter like cold cream at the corners. After the greetings usual between a chief and one of his headmen together with whom, from the retreat in the mopane forest where they lay together in the same age-group recovering from circumcision, he had long ago emerged a man, the chief said, 'When is your son coming back?'

'I have no news.'

'Did he sign for the mines?'

'No.'

'He's gone to the tobacco farms?'

'He didn't tell us.'

'Gone away to find work and doesn't tell his mother? What sort of child is that? Didn't you teach him?'

The goats were tongue-ing three hunchback bushes that were all that was left of a hedge round the chief's house. The man took out a round tin dented with child's tooth-marks and taking care not to spill any snuff, dosed himself. He gestured at the beasts, for permission: 'They're eating up your house . . . ' He made a move towards the necessity to drive them on.

'There is nothing left there to eat.' The chief ignored his hedge, planted by his oldest wife who had been to school at the mission up the river. He stood among the goats as if he would ask more questions. Then he turned and went back to his yard, dismissing himself. The other man watched. It seemed he might call after; but instead drove his animals with the familiar cries, this time unnecessarily loud and frequent.

Often an army patrol Land Rover came to the village. No one could predict when this would be because it was not possible to count the days in between and be sure that so many would elapse before it returned, as could be done in the case of a tax-collector or cattle-dipping officer. But it could be heard minutes away, crashing through the mopane like a frightened animal, and dust hung marking the direction from which it was coming. The children ran to tell. The women went from hut to hut. One of the chief's wives would enjoy the importance of bearing the news: 'The government is coming to see you.' He would be out of his house when the Land Rover stopped and a black soldier (murmuring towards the chief the required respectful greeting in their own language) jumped out and opened the door for the white soldier. The white soldier had learned the names of all the local chiefs. He gave greetings with white men's brusqueness: 'Everything all right?' And the chief repeated to him: 'Everything is all right.' 'No one been bothering you in this village?' 'No one is troubling us.' But the white soldier signalled to his black men and they went through every hut busy as wives when they are cleaning, turning

91

over bedding, thrusting gun-butts into the pile of ash and rubbish where the chickens searched, even looking in, their eyes dazzled by darkness, to the hut where one of the old women who had gone crazy had to be kept most of the time. The white soldier stood beside the Land Rover waiting for them. He told the chief of things that were happening not far from the village; not far at all. The road that passed five kilometres away had been blown up. 'Someone plants land-mines in the road and as soon as we repair it they put them there again. Those people come from across the river and they pass this way. They wreck our vehicles and kill people.'

The heads gathered round weaved as if at the sight of bodies laid there horrifyingly before them.

'They will kill you, too – burn your huts, all of you – if you let them stay with you.'

A woman turned her face away: 'Aïe-aïe-aïe-aïe.'

His forefinger half-circled his audience. 'I'm telling you. You'll see what they do.'


The chief's latest wife, taken only the year before and of the age-group of his elder grandchildren, had not come out to listen to the white man. But she heard from others what he had said, and fiercely smoothing her legs with grease, demanded of the chief, 'Why does he want us to die, that white man?'

Her husband, who had just been a passionately shuddering lover, became at once one of the important old with whom she did not count and could not argue. 'You talk about things you don't know. Don't speak for the sake of making a noise.'

To punish him, she picked up the strong, young girl's baby she had borne him and went out of the room where she slept with him on the big bed that had come down the river by barge, before the army's machine guns were pointing at the other bank.

He appeared at his mother's hut. There, the middle-aged man on whom the villagers depended, to whom the government looked when it wanted taxes paid and culling orders carried out, became a son – the ageless category, no matter from which age-group to another he passed in the progression of her life and his. The old woman was at her toilet. The great weight of her body settled around her where she sat on a reed mat outside the door. He pushed a stool under himself. Set out was a small mirror with a pink plastic frame and stand, in which he caught sight of his face, screwed up. A large black comb; a little carved box inlaid with red lucky beans she had always had, he used to beg to be allowed to play with it fifty years ago. He waited, not so much out of respect as in the bond of indifference to all outside their mutual contact that reasserts itself when lions and their kin lie against one another.

She cocked a glance, swinging the empty loops of her stretched ear-lobes. He did not say what he had come for.

She had chosen a tiny bone spoon from the box and was poking with trembling care up each round hole of distended nostril. She cleaned the crust of dried snot and dust from her delicate instrument and flicked the dirt in the direction away from him.

She said: 'Do you know where your sons are?'

'Yes, I know where my sons are. You have seen three of them here today. Two are in school at the mission. The baby – he's with the mother.' A slight smile, to which the old woman did not respond. Her preferences among the sons had no connection with sexual pride.

'Good. You can be glad of all that. But don't ask other people about theirs.'

As often when people who share the same blood share the same thought, for a moment mother and son looked exactly alike, he old-womanish, she mannish.

'If the ones we know are missing, there are not always empty places,' he said.

She stirred consideringly in her bulk. Leaned back to regard him: 'It used to be that all children were our own children. All sons our sons. *Old-fashion*, these people here' – the hard English word rolled out of their language like a pebble, and came to rest where aimed, at his feet.


It was spring: the mopane leaves turn, drying up and dying, spattering the sand with blood and rust – a battlefield, it must have looked, from the patrol planes. In August there is no rain to come for two months yet. Nothing grows but the flies hatch. The heat rises daily and the nights hold it, without a stir, till morning. On these nights the radio voice carried so clearly it could be heard from the chief's house all through the village. Many were being captured in the bush and killed by the army – *seek and destroy* was what the white men said now – and many in the army were being set upon in the bush or blown up in their trucks and buried with full military honours. This was expected to continue until October because the men in the bush knew that it was their last chance before the rains came and chained their feet in mud.

On these hot nights when people cannot sleep anyway, beer-drinks last until very late. People drink more; the women know this, and brew more. There is a fire but no one sits close round it.

Without a moon the dark is thick with heat; when the moon is full the dark shimmers thinly in a hot mirage off the river. Black faces are blue, there are watermarks along noses and biceps. The chief sat on his chair and wore shoes and socks in spite of the heat; those drinking nearest him could smell the suffering of his feet. The planes of jaw and lips he noticed in moonlight molten over them, moonlight pouring moths broken from white cases on the mopane and mosquitoes rising from the river, pouring glory like the light in the religious pictures people got at the mission – he had seen those faces about lately in the audacity of day, as well. An ox had been killed and there was the scent of meat sizzling in the village (just look at the behaviour of the dogs, they knew) although there was no marriage or other festival that called for someone to slaughter one of his beasts. When the chief allowed himself, at last, to meet the eyes of a stranger, the whites that had been showing at an oblique angle disappeared and he took rather than saw the full gaze of the seeing eye: the pupils with their defiance, their belief, their claim, hold, on him. He let it happen only once. For the rest, he saw their arrogant lifted jaws to each other and warrior smiles to the girls, as they drank. The children were drawn to them, fighting one another silently for places close up. Towards midnight – his watch had its own glowing galaxy – he left his chair and did not come back from the shadows where men went to urinate. Often at beer-drinks the chief would go home while others were still drinking.

He went to his brick house whose roof shone almost bright as day. He did not go to the room where his new wife and sixth son would be sleeping in the big bed, but simply took from the kitchen, where it was kept when not in use, a bicycle belonging to one of his hangers-on, relative or retainer. He wheeled it away from the huts in the clearing, his village and grandfather's village that disappeared so quickly behind him in the mopane, and began to ride through the sand. He was not afraid he would meet a patrol and be shot; alone at night in the sand forest, the forested desert he had known before and would know beyond his span of life, he didn't believe in the power of a roving band of government men to end that life. The going was heavy but he had mastered when young the art of riding on this, the only terrain he knew, and the ability came back. In an hour he arrived at the army post, called out who he was to the sentry with a machine gun, and had to wait, like a beggar rather than a chief, to be allowed to approach and be searched. There were black soldiers on duty but they woke the white man. It was the one who knew his name, his clan, his village, the way these modern white men were taught. He seemed to know at once why the chief had come; frowning in concentration to grasp details, his mouth was open in a smile and the point of his tongue curled touching at back teeth the way a man will verify facts one by one on his fingers. 'How many?'

'Six or ten or – but sometimes it's only, say, three or one . . . I don't know. One is here, he's gone; they come again.'

'They take food, they sleep, and off. Yes. They make the people give them what they want, that's it, eh? And you know who it is who hides them – who shows them where to sleep – of course you know.'

The chief sat on one of the chairs in that place, the army's place, and the white soldier was standing. 'Who is it – ' the chief was having difficulty in saying what he wanted in English, he had the feeling it was not coming out as he had meant nor being understood as he had expected. 'I can't know who is it' – a hand moved restlessly, he held a breath and released it – 'in the village there's many, plenty people. If it's this one or this one – ' He stopped, shaking his head with a reminder to the white man of his authority, which the white soldier was quick to placate. 'Of course. Never mind. They frighten the people; the people can't say no. They kill people who say no, 'eh; cut their ears off, you know that? Tear away their lips. Don't you see the pictures in the papers?'

'We never saw it. I heard the government say on the radio.'

'They're still drinking . . . How long – an hour ago?'

The white soldier checked with a look the other men, whose stance had changed to that of bodies ready to break into movement: grab weapons, run, fling themselves at the Land Rovers guarded in the dark outside. He picked up the telephone receiver but blocked the mouth-piece as if it were someone about to make an objection. 'Chief, I'll be with you in a moment. – Take him to the duty room and make coffee. Just wait – ' he leaned his full reach towards a drawer in a cabinet on the left of the desk and, scrabbling to get it open, took out a half-full bottle of brandy. Behind the chief's back he gestured the bottle towards the chief, and a black soldier jumped obediently to take it.


The chief went to a cousin's house in a village the other side of the army post later that night. He said he had been to a beer-drink and could not ride home because of the white men's curfew.

The white soldier had instructed that he should not be in his own village when the arrests were made so that he could not be connected with these and would not be in danger of having his ears cut off for taking heed of what the government wanted of him, or having his lips mutilated for what he had told.

His cousin gave him blankets. He slept in a hut with her father. The deaf old man was aware neither that he had come nor was leaving so early that last night's moon, the size of the bicycle's reflector, was still shiny in the sky. The bicycle rode up on springhares without disturbing them, in the forest; there was a stink of jackal-fouling still sharp on the dew. Smoke already marked his village; early cooking fires were lit. Then he saw that the smoke, the black particles spindling at his face, were not from cooking fires. Instead of going faster as he pumped his feet against the weight of sand the bicycle seemed to slow along with his mind, to find in each revolution of its wheels the countersurge: to stop; not go on. But there was no way not to reach what he found. The planes only children bothered to look up at any longer had come in the night and dropped something terrible and alive that no one could have read or heard about enough to be sufficiently afraid of. He saw first a bloody kaross, a dog caught on the roots of an upturned tree. The earth under the village seemed to have burst open and flung away what it carried: the huts, pots, gourds, blankets, the tin trunks, alarm-clocks, curtain-booth photographs, bicycles, radios and shoes brought back from the mines, the bright cloths young wives wound on their heads, the pretty pictures of white lambs and pink children at the knees of the golden-haired Christ the Scottish Mission Board first brought long ago – all five generations of the clan's life that had been chronicled by each succeeding generation in episodes told to the next. The huts had staved in like broken anthills. Within earth walls baked and streaked by fire the thatch and roof-poles were ash. He bellowed and stumbled from hut to hut, nothing answered frenzy, not even a chicken rose from under his feet. The walls of his house still stood. It was gutted and the roof had buckled. A black stiff creature lay roasted on its chain in the yard. In one of the huts he saw a human shape transformed the same way, a thing of stiff tar daubed on a recognisable framework. It was the hut where the mad woman lived; when those who had survived fled, they had forgotten her.

The chief's mother and his youngest wife were not among them. But the baby boy lived, and will grow up in the care of the older wives. No one can say what it was the white soldier said over the telephone to his commanding officer, and if the commanding officer had told him what was going to be done, or whether the white soldier knew, as a matter of procedure laid down in his military training for this kind of war, what would be done. The chief hanged himself in the mopane. The police or the army (much the same these days, people confuse them) found the bicycle

97

beneath his dangling shoes. So the family hanger-on still rides it; it would have been lost if it had been safe in the kitchen when the raid came. No one knows where the chief found a rope, in the ruins of his village.

The people are beginning to go back. The dead are properly buried in ancestral places in the mopane forest. The women are to be seen carrying tins and grain panniers of mud up from the river. In talkative bands they squat and smear, raising the huts again. They bring sheaves of reeds exceeding their own height, balanced like the cross-stroke of a majuscular T on their heads. The men's voices sound through the mopane as they choose and fell trees for the roof supports.

A white flag on a mopane pole hangs outside the house whose white walls, built like a white man's, stand from before this time.

# At the Rendezvous of Victory

A young black boy used to brave the dogs in white men's suburbs to deliver telegrams; Sinclair 'General Giant' Zwedu has those bite scars on his legs to this day.

So goes the opening paragraph of a 'profile' copyrighted by a British Sunday paper, reprinted by reciprocal agreement with papers in New York and Washington, syndicated as far as Australia and translated in both *Le Monde* and *Neue Züricher Zeitung*.

But like everything else he was to read about himself, it was not quite like that. No. Ever since he was a kid he loved dogs, and those dogs who chased the bicycle – he just used to whistle in his way at them, and they would stand there wagging their long tails and feeling silly. The scars on his legs were from wounds received when the white commando almost captured him, blew up one of his hideouts in the bush. But he understood why the journalist had decided to paint the wounds over as dog-bites – it made a kind of novel opening to the story, and it showed at once that the journalist wasn't on the side of the whites. It was true that he who became Sinclair 'General Giant' Zwedu was born in the blacks' compound on a white man's sugar farm in the hottest and most backward part of the country, and that, after only a few years at a school where children drew their sums in the dust, he was the post office messenger in the farmers' town. It was in that two-street town, with the whites' Central Hotel, Main Road Garage, Buyrite Stores, Snooker Club and railhead, that he first heard the voice of the brother who was to become prime minister and president, a voice from a big trumpet on the top of a shabby van. It summoned him (there were others, but they didn't become anybody) to a meeting in the Catholic Mission Hall in Goodwill Township –

which was what the white farmers called the black shanty town outside their own. And it was here, in Goodwill Township, that the young post office messenger took away the local Boy Scout troop organised by but segregated from the white Boy Scout troop in the farmers' town, and transformed the scouts into the Youth Group of the National Independence Party. Yes – he told them – you will be prepared. The Party will teach you how to make a fire the government can't put out.

It was he who, when the leaders of the Party were detained for the first time, was imprisoned with the future prime minister and became one of his chief lieutenants. He, in fact, who in jail made up defiance songs that soon were being sung at mass meetings, who imitated the warders, made pregnant one of the women prisoners who polished the cell floors (though no one believed her when she proudly displayed the child as his, he would have known *that* was true), and finally, when he was sent to another prison in order to remove his invigorating influence from fellow political detainees, overpowered three warders and escaped across the border.

It was this exploit that earned him the title 'General Giant' as prophets, saints, rogues and heroes receive theirs: named by the anonymous talk of ordinary people. He did not come back until he had wintered in the unimaginable cold of countries that offer refuge and military training, gone to rich desert cities to ask for money from the descendants of people who had sold Africans as slaves, and to the island where sugar-cane workers, as his mother and father had been, were now powerful enough to supply arms. He was with the first band of men who had left home with empty hands, on bare feet, and came back with AKM assault rifles, heat-guided missiles and limpet mines.

The future prime minister was imprisoned again and again and finally fled the country and established the Party's leadership in exile. When Sinclair 'General Giant' met him in London or Algiers, the future prime minister wore a dark suit whose close weave was midnight blue in the light. He himself wore a bush outfit that originally had been put together by men who lived less like men than prides of lion, tick-ridden, thirsty, waiting in

100

thickets of thorn. As these men increased in numbers and boldness, and he rose in command of them, the outfit elaborated into a combat uniform befitting his style, title and achievement. At the beginning of the war, he had led a ragged hit-and-run group; after four years and the deaths of many, which emphasised his giant indestructibility, his men controlled a third of the country and he was the man the white army wanted most to capture.

Before the future prime minister talked to the Organisation of African Unity or United Nations he had now to send for and consult with his commander-in-chief of the liberation army, Sinclair 'General Giant' Zwedu. General Giant came from the bush in his Czech jeep, in a series of tiny planes from secret airstrips, and at last would board a scheduled jet liner among oil and mineral men who thought they were sitting beside just another dolled-up black official from some unheard-of state whose possibilities they might have to look into sometime. When the consultation in the foreign capital was over, General Giant did not fidget long in the putter of official cocktail parties, but would disappear to find for himself whatever that particular capital could offer to meet his high capacities – for leading men to fight without fear, exciting people to caper, shout with pleasure, drink and argue; for touching women. After a night in a bar and a bed with girls (he never had to pay professionals, always found well-off, respectable women, black or white, whose need for delights simply matched his own) he would take a plane back to Africa. He never wanted to linger. He never envied his brother, the future prime minister, his flat in London and the invitations to country houses to discuss the future of the country. He went back imperatively as birds migrate to Africa to mate and assure the survival of their kind, journeying thousands of miles, just as he flew and drove deeper and deeper into where he belonged until he reached again his headquarters – that the white commandos often claimed to have destroyed but could not be destroyed because his headquarters were the bush itself.

The war would not have been won without General Giant. At the Peace Conference he took no part in the deliberations but was there at his brother's, the future prime minister's side: a deterrent

101

weapon, a threat to the defeated white government of what would happen if peace were not made. Now and then he cleared his throat of a constriction of boredom; the white delegates were alarmed as if he had roared.

Constitutional talks went on for many weeks; there was a cease-fire, of course. He wanted to go back – to his headquarters – home – but one of the conditions of the cease-fire had been that he should be withdrawn 'from the field' as the official term, coined in wars fought over poppy-meadows, phrased it. He wandered about London. He went to nightclubs and was invited to join parties of Arabs who, he found, had no idea where the country he had fought for, and won for his people, was; this time he really did roar – with laughter. He walked through Soho but couldn't understand why anyone would like to watch couples making the movements of love-making on the cinema screen instead of doing it themselves. He came upon the Natural History Museum in South Kensington and was entranced by the life that existed anterior to his own unthinking familiarity with ancient nature hiding the squat limpet mines, the iron clutches of offensive and defensive hand-grenades, the angular AKMs, metal blue with heat. He sent postcards of mammoths and gasteropods to his children, who were still where they had been with his wife all through the war – in the black location of the capital of his home country. Since she was his wife, she had been under police surveillance, and detained several times, but had survived by saying she and her husband were separated. Which was true, in a way; a man leading a guerrilla war has no family, he must forget about meals cooked for him by a woman, nights in a bed with two places hollowed by their bodies, and the snuffle of a baby close by. He made love to a black singer from Jamaica, not young, whose style was a red-head wig rather than fashionable rigid pigtails. She composed a song about his bravery in the war in a country she imagined but had never seen, and sang it at a victory rally where all the brothers in exile as well as the white sympathisers with their cause, applauded her. In her flat she had a case of special Scotch whisky, twelve years old, sent by an admirer. She said – sang to him – Let's not let it get any older. As she worked only at night, they spent whole days indoors making love when the weather was bad – the big man, General Giant, was like a poor stray cat, in the cold rain: he would walk on the balls of shoe-soles, shaking each foot as he lifted it out of the wet.

He was waiting for the okay, as he said to his brother, the future prime minister, to go back to their country and take up his position as commander-in-chief of the new state's Defence Force. His title would become an official rank, the highest, like that of army chiefs in Britain and the United States – General Zwedu.

His brother turned solemn, dark in his mind; couldn't be followed there. He said the future of the army was a tremendous problem at present under discussion. The two armies, black and white, who had fought each other, would have to be made one. What the discussions were also about remained in the dark: the defeated white government, the European powers by whom the new black state was promised loans for reconstruction, had insisted that Sinclair 'General Giant' Zwedu be relieved of all military authority. His personality was too strong and too strongly associated with the triumph of the freedom fighter army for him to be anything but a divisive reminder of the past, in the new, regular army. Let him stand for parliament in the first peace-time election, his legend would guarantee that he win the seat. Then the prime minister could find him some safe portfolio.

What portfolio? What? This was in the future prime minister's mind when General Giant couldn't follow him. 'What he knows how to do is defend our country, that he fought for,' the future prime minister said to the trusted advisers, British lawyers and African experts from American universities. And while he was saying it, the others knew he did not want, could not have his brother Sinclair 'General Giant' Zwedu, that master of the wilderness, breaking the confinement of peace-time barracks.

He left him in Europe on some hastily-invented mission until the independence celebrations. Then he brought him home to the old colonial capital that was now theirs, and at the airport wept with triumph and anguish in his arms, while schoolchildren sang. He gave him a portfolio – Sport and Recreation; harmless.

General Giant looked at his big hands as if the appointment

were an actual object, held there. What was he supposed to do with it? The great lungs that pumped his organ-voice failed; he spoke flatly, kindly, almost pityingly to his brother, the prime minister.

Now they both wore dark blue suits. At first, he appeared prominently at the prime minister's side as a tacit recompense, to show the people that he was still acknowledged by the prime minister as a co-founder of the nation, and its popular hero. He had played football on a patch of bare earth between wattle-branch goal posts on the sugar farm, as a child, and as a youth on a stretch of waste ground near the Catholic Mission Hall; as a man he had been at war, without time for games. In the first few months he rather enjoyed attending important matches in his official capacity, watching from a special box and later seeing himself sitting there, on a TV newsreel. It was a Sunday, a holiday amusement; the holiday went on too long. There was not much obligation to make speeches, in his cabinet post, but because his was a name known over the world, his place reserved in the mountain stronghold Valhalla of guerrilla wars, journalists went to him for statements on all kinds of issues. Besides, he was splendid copy, talkative, honest, indiscreet and emotional. Again and again, he embarrassed his government by giving an outrageous opinion, that contradicted government policy, on problems that were none of his business. The Party caucus reprimanded him again and again. He responded by seldom turning up at caucus meetings. The caucus members said that Zwedu (it was time his 'title' was dropped) thought too much of himself and had taken offence. Again, he knew that what was assumed was not quite true. He was bored with the caucus. He wanted to yawn all the time, he said, like a hippopotamus with its huge jaws open in the sun, half-asleep, in the thick brown water of the river near his last headquarters. The prime minister laughed at this, and they drank together with arms round one another – as they did in the old days in the Youth Group. The prime minister told him – 'But seriously, sport and recreation are very important in building up our nation. For the next budget, I'll see that there's a bigger grant to your department, you'll be able to plan. You know how to inspire young men . . . I'm told a local team has adapted one of the freedom songs you made up, they sang it on TV.'

The minister of Sport and Recreation sent his deputy to officiate at sports meetings these days and he didn't hear his war song become a football fans' chant. The Jamaican singer had arrived on an engagement at the Hilton that had just opened conference rooms, bars, a casino and nightclub on a site above the town where the old colonial prison used to be (the new prison was on the site of the former Peace Corps camp). He was there in the nightclub every night, drinking the brand of Scotch she had had in her London flat, tilting his head while she sang. The hotel staff pointed him out to overseas visitors – Sinclair 'General Giant' Zwedu, the General Giap, the Che Guevara of a terrible war there'd been in this country. The tourists had spent the day, taken by private plane, viewing game in what the travel brochure described as the country's magnificent game park but – the famous freedom fighter could have told them – wasn't quite that; was in fact his territory, his headquarters. Sometimes he danced with one of the women, their white teeth contrasting with shiny sunburned skin almost as if they had been black. Once there was some sort of row; he danced too many times with a woman who appeared to be enjoying this intimately, and her husband objected. The 'convivial minister' had laughed, taken the man by the scruff of his white linen jacket and dropped him back in his chair, a local journalist reported, but the government-owned local press did not print his story or picture. An overseas journalist interviewed 'General Giant' on the pretext of the incident, and got from him (the minister was indeed convivial, entertaining the journalist to excellent whisky in the house he had rented for the Jamaican singer) some opinions on matters far removed from nightclub scandal.

When questions were asked in parliament about an article in an American weekly on the country's international alliances, 'General Giant' stood up and, again, gave expression to convictions the local press could not print. He said that the defence of the country might have been put in the hands of neo-colonialists

105

who had been the country's enemies during the war – and he was powerless to do anything about that. But he would take the law into his own hands to protect the National Independence Party's principles of a people's democracy (he used the old name, on this occasion, although it had been shortened to National Party). Hadn't he fought, hadn't the brothers spilled their blood to get rid of the old laws and the old bosses, that made them *nothing*? Hadn't they fought for new laws under which they would be men? He would shed blood rather than see the Party betrayed in the name of so-called rational alliances and national unity.

International advisers to the government thought the speech, if inflammatory, so confused it might best be ignored. Members of the cabinet and members of parliament wanted the prime minister to get rid of him. General Giant Zwedu? How? Where to? Extreme anger was always expressed by the prime minister in the form of extreme sorrow. He was angry with both his cabinet members and his comrade, without whom they would never have been sitting in the House of Assembly. He sent for Zwedu. (He must accept that name now; he simply refused to accommodate himself to anything, he illogically wouldn't even drop the 'Sinclair' though *that* was the name of the white sugar farmer his parents had worked for, and nobody kept those slave names any more.)

Zwedu: so at ease and handsome in his cabinet minister's suit (it was not the old blue, but a pin-stripe flannel the Jamaican singer had ordered at his request, and brought from London), one could not believe wild and dangerous words could come out of his mouth. He looked good enough for a diplomatic post somewhere . . . Unthinkable. The prime minister, full of sorrow and silences, told him he must stop drinking. He must stop giving interviews. There was no mention of the ministry; the prime minister did not tell his brother he would not give in to pressure to take that away from him, the cabinet post he had never wanted but that was all there was to offer. He would not take it away – at least not until this could be done decently under cover of a cabinet reshuffle. The prime minister had to say to his brother, you mustn't let me down. What he wanted to say was: What have I done to you?

There was a crop failure and trouble with the unions on the coal mines; by the time the cabinet reshuffle came the press hardly noticed that a minister of Sport and Recreation had been replaced. Mr Sinclair Zwedu was not given an alternative portfolio, but he was referred to as a former minister when his name was added to the boards of multinational industrial firms instructed by their principals to Africanise. He could be counted upon not to appear at those meetings, either. His director's fees paid for cases of whisky, but sometimes went to his wife, to whom he had never returned, and the teenage children with whom he would suddenly appear in the best stores of the town, buying whatever they silently pointed at. His old friends blamed the Jamaican woman, not the prime minister, for his disappearance from public life. She went back to England – her reasons were sexual and honest, she realised she was too old for him – but his way of life did not recover; could not recover the war, the third of the country's territory that had been his domain when the white government had lost control to him, and the black government did not yet exist.

The country is open to political and trade missions from both East and West, now, instead of these being confined to allies of the old white government. The airport has been extended. The new departure lounge is a sculpture gallery with reclining figures among potted plants, wearily waiting for connections to places whose directions criss-cross the colonial North-South compass of communication. A former chief-of-staff of the white army, who, since the black government came to power, has been retained as chief military adviser to the defence ministry, recently spent some hours in the lounge waiting for a plane that was to take him on a government mission to Europe. He was joined by a journalist booked on the same flight home to London, after a rather disappointing return visit to the country. Well, he remarked to the military man as they drank vodka-and-tonic together, who wants to read about rice-growing schemes instead of seek-and-destroy raids? This was a graceful reference to the ex-chief-of-staff's successes with that strategy at the beginning of the war, a reference safe in the cosy no-man's-land of a departure lounge, out

107

of earshot of the new black security officials alert to any hint of encouragement of an old-guard white coup.

A musical gong preceded announcements of the new estimated departure time of the delayed British Airways plane. A swami found sweets somewhere in his saffron robes and went among the travellers handing out comfits with a message of peace and love. Businessmen used the opportunity to write reports on briefcases opened on their knees. Black children were spores attached to maternal skirts. White children ran back and forth to the bar counter, buying potato crips and peanuts. The journalist insisted on another round of drinks.

Every now and then the departure of some other flight was called and the display of groups and single figures would change; some would leave, while a fresh surge would be let in through the emigration barriers and settle in a new composition. Those who were still waiting for delayed planes became part of the permanent collection, so to speak; they included a Canadian evangelical party who read their gospels with the absorption other people gave to paperback thrillers, a very old black woman dry as the fish in her woven carrier, and a prosperous black couple, elegantly dressed. The ex-chief-of-staff and his companion were sitting not far behind these two, who flirted and caressed, like whites – it was quite unusual to see those people behaving that way in public. Both the white men noticed this although they were able to observe only the back of the man's head and the profile of the girl, pretty, painted, shameless as she licked his tiny black ear and lazily tickled, with long fingers on the stilts of purple nails, the roll of his neck.

The ex-chief-of-staff made no remark, was not interested – what did one *not* see, in the country, now that they had taken over. The journalist was the man who had written a profile, just after the war: *a young black boy used to brave the dogs in white men's suburbs* . . . Suddenly he leant forward, staring at the back of the black man's head. 'That's General Giant! I know those ears!' He got up and went over to the bar, turning casually at the counter to examine the couple from the front. He bought two more vodka-and-tonics, swiftly was back to his companion, the ice chuntering in the glasses. 'It's him. I thought so. I used to know him well. Him, all right. Fat! Wearing suède shoes. And the tart . . . where'd he find her?'

The ex-chief-of-staff's uniform, his thick wad of campaign ribbons over the chest and cap thrust down to his fine eyebrows, seemed to defend him against the heat rather than make him suffer, but the journalist felt confused and stifled as the vodka came out distilled once again in sweat and he did not know whether he should or should not simply walk up to 'General Giant' (no secretaries or security men to get past, now) and ask for an interview. Would anyone want to read it? Could he sell it anywhere? A distraction that made it difficult for him to make up his mind was the public address system nagging that the two passengers holding up flight something-or-other were requested to board the aircraft immediately. No one stirred. 'General Giant' (no mistaking him) simply signalled, a big hand snapping in the air, when he wanted fresh drinks for himself and his girl, and the barman hopped to it, although the bar was self-service. Before the journalist could come to a decision an air hostess ran in with the swish of stockings chafing thigh past thigh and stopped angrily, looking down at the black couple. The journalist could not hear what was said, but she stood firm while the couple took their time getting up, the girl letting her arm slide languidly off the man; laughing, arranging their hand luggage on each other's shoulders.

Where was he *taking* her?

The girl put one high-heeled sandal down in front of the other, as a model negotiates a catwalk. Sinclair 'General Giant' Zwedu followed her backside the way a man follows a paid woman, with no thought of her in his closed, shiny face, and the ex-chief-of-staff and the journalist did not know whether he recognised them, even saw them, as he passed without haste, letting the plane wait for him.

# The Ultimate Safari

'THE AFRICAN ADVENTURE LIVES ON . . . YOU CAN DO IT! THE
ULTIMATE SAFARI OR EXPEDITION WITH LEADERS WHO KNOW
AFRICA.'

*Travel advertisement,* Observer, *27 November 1988*

That night our mother went to the shop and she didn't come back.
Ever. What happened? I don't know. My father also had gone
away one day and never come back; but he was fighting in the
war. We were in the war, too, but we were children, we were like
our grandmother and grandfather, we didn't have guns. The
people my father was fighting – the bandits, they are called by our
government – ran all over the place and we ran away from them
like chickens chased by dogs. We didn't know where to go. Our
mother went to the shop because someone said you could get some
oil for cooking. We were happy because we hadn't tasted oil for a
long time; perhaps she got the oil and someone knocked her down
in the dark and took that oil from her. Perhaps she met the
bandits. If you meet them, they will kill you. Twice they came to
our village and we ran and hid in the bush and when they'd gone
we came back and found they had taken everything; but the third
time they came back there was nothing to take, no oil, no food, so
they burned the thatch and the roofs of our houses fell in. My
mother found some pieces of tin and we put those up over part of
the house. We were waiting there for her that night she never came
back.

We were frightened to go out, even to do our business, because
the bandits did come. Not into our house – without a roof it must
have looked as if there was no one in it, everything gone – but all

110

through the village. We heard people screaming and running. We were afraid even to run, without our mother to tell us where. I am the middle one, the girl, and my little brother clung against my stomach with his arms round my neck and his legs round my waist like a baby monkey to its mother. All night my first-born brother kept in his hand a broken piece of wood from one of our burnt house-poles. It was to save himself if the bandits found him.

We stayed there all day. Waiting for her. I don't know what day it was; there was no school, no church any more in our village, so you didn't know whether it was a Sunday or a Monday.

When the sun was going down, our grandmother and grandfather came. Someone from our village had told them we children were alone, our mother had not come back. I say 'grandmother' before 'grandfather' because it's like that: our grandmother is big and strong, not yet old, and our grandfather is small, you don't know where he is, in his loose trousers, he smiles but he hasn't heard what you're saying, and his hair looks as if he's left it full of soap suds. Our grandmother took us – me, the baby, my first-born brother, our grandfather – back to her house and we were all afraid (except the baby, asleep on our grandmother's back) of meeting the bandits on the way. We waited a long time at our grandmother's place. Perhaps it was a month. We were hungry. Our mother never came. While we were waiting for her to fetch us, our grandmother had no food for us, no food for our grandfather and herself. A woman with milk in her breasts gave us some for my little brother, although at our house he used to eat porridge, same as we did. Our grandmother took us to look for wild spinach but everyone else in the village did the same and there wasn't a leaf left.

Our grandfather, walking a little behind some young men, went to look for our mother but didn't find her. Our grandmother cried with other women and I sang the hymns with them. They brought a little food – some beans – but after two days there was nothing again. Our grandfather used to have three sheep and a cow and a vegetable garden but the bandits had long ago taken the sheep and the cow, because they were hungry, too; and when planting time came our grandfather had no seed to plant.

111

So they decided – our grandmother did; our grandfather made little noises and rocked from side to side, but she took no notice – we would go away. We children were pleased. We wanted to go away from where our mother wasn't and where we were hungry. We wanted to go where there were no bandits and there was food. We were glad to think there must be such a place; away.


Our grandmother gave her church clothes to someone in exchange for some dried mealies and she boiled them and tied them in a rag. We took them with us when we went and she thought we would get water from the rivers but we didn't come to any river and we got so thirsty we had to turn back. Not all the way to our grandparents' place but to a village where there was a pump. She opened the basket where she carried some clothes and the mealies and she sold her shoes to buy a big plastic container for water. I said, *Gogo*, how will you go to church now even without shoes, but she said we had a long journey and too much to carry. At that village we met other people who were also going away. We joined them because they seemed to know where that was better than we did.

To get there we had to go through the Kruger Park. We knew about the Kruger Park. A kind of whole country of animals – elephants, lions, jackals, hyenas, hippos, crocodiles, all kinds of animals. We had some of them in our own country, before the war (our grandfather remembers; we children weren't born yet) but the bandits kill the elephants and sell their tusks, and the bandits and our soldiers have eaten all the buck. There was a man in our village without legs – a crocodile took them off, in our river; but all the same our country is a country of people, not animals. We knew about the Kruger Park because some of our men used to leave home to work there in the places where white people came to stay and look at the animals.


So we started to go away again. There were women and other children like me who had to carry the small ones on their backs when the women got tired. A man led us into the Kruger Park: are

112

we there yet, are we there yet, I kept asking our grandmother. Not yet, the man said, when she asked him for me. He told us we had to take a long way to get round the fence, which he explained would kill you, roast off your skin the moment you touched it, like the wires high up on poles that give electric light in our towns. I've seen that sign of a head without ears or skin or hair on an iron box at the mission hospital we used to have before it was blown up.

When I asked the next time, they said we'd been walking in the Kruger Park for an hour. But it looked just like the bush we'd been walking through all day, and we hadn't seen any animals except the monkeys and birds which live around us at home, and a tortoise that, of course, couldn't get away from us. My first-born brother and the other boys brought it to the man so it could be killed and we could cook and eat it. He let it go because he told us we could not make a fire; all the time we were in the Park we must not make a fire because the smoke would show we were there. Police, wardens, would come and send us back where we came from. He said we must move like animals among the animals, away from the roads, away from the white people's camps. And at that moment I heard – I'm sure I was the first to hear – cracking branches and the sound of something parting grasses and I almost squealed because I thought it was the police, wardens – the people he was telling us to look out for – who had found us already. And it was an elephant, and another elephant, and more elephants, big blots of dark moved wherever you looked between the trees. They were curling their trunks round the red leaves of the mopane trees and stuffing them into their mouths. The babies leaned against their mothers. The almost grown-up ones wrestled like my first-born brother with his friends – only they used trunks instead of arms. I was so interested I forgot to be afraid. The man said we should just stand still and be quiet while the elephants passed. They passed very slowly because elephants are too big to need to run from anyone.

The buck ran from us. They jumped so high they seemed to fly. The wart-hogs stopped dead, when they heard us, and swerved off the way a boy in our village used to zigzag on the bicycle his father had brought back from the mines. We followed the animals to where they drank. When they had gone, we went to their waterholes. We were never thirsty without finding water, but the animals ate, ate all the time. Whenever you saw them they were eating, grass, trees, roots. And there was nothing for us. The mealies were finished. The only food we could eat was what the baboons ate, dry little figs full of ants, that grow along the branches of the trees at the rivers. It was hard to be like the animals.

When it was very hot during the day we would find lions lying asleep. They were the colour of the grass and we didn't see them at first but the man did, and he led us back and a long way round where they slept. I wanted to lie down like the lions. My little brother was getting thin but he was very heavy. When our grandmother looked for me, to put him on my back, I tried not to see. My first-born brother stopped talking; and when we rested he had to be shaken to get up again, as if he was just like our grandfather, he couldn't hear. I saw flies crawling on our grandmother's face and she didn't brush them off; I was frightened. I picked up a palm leaf and chased them.


We walked at night as well as by day. We could see the fires where the white people were cooking in the camps and we could smell the smoke and the meat. We watched the hyenas with their backs that slope as if they're ashamed, slipping through the bush after the smell. If one turned its head, you saw it had big brown shining eyes like our own, when we looked at each other in the dark. The wind brought voices in our own language from the compounds where the people who work in the camps live. A woman among us wanted to go to them at night and ask them to help us. They can give us the food from the dustbins, she said, she started wailing and our grandmother had to grab her and put a hand over her mouth. The men who led us had told us that we must keep out of the way of our people who worked at the Kruger Park; if they helped us they would lose their work. If they saw us, all they could do was pretend we were not there; they had seen only animals. Sometimes we stopped to sleep for a little while at night. We slept close together. I don't know which night it was – because we were walking, walking, any time, all the time – we heard the lions very near. Not groaning loudly the way they did far off. Panting, like we do when we run, but it's a different kind of panting: you can hear they're not running, they're waiting, somewhere near. We all rolled closer together, on top of each other, the ones on the edge fighting to get into the middle. I was squashed against a woman who smelled bad because she was afraid but I was glad to hold tight on to her. I prayed to God to make the lions take someone on the edge and go. I shut my eyes not to see the tree from which a lion might jump right into the middle of us, where I was. The man who led us jumped up instead, and beat on the tree with a dead branch. He had taught us never to make a sound but he shouted. He shouted at the lions like a drunk man shouting at nobody in our village. The lions went away. We heard them groaning, shouting back at him from far off.

We were tired, so tired. My first-born brother and the man had to lift our grandfather from stone to stone where we found places to cross the rivers. Our grandmother is strong but her feet were bleeding. We could not carry the basket on our heads any longer, we couldn't carry anything except my little brother. We left our things under a bush. As long as our bodies get there, our grandmother said. Then we ate some wild fruit we didn't know from home and our stomachs ran. We were in the grass called elephant grass because it is nearly as tall as an elephant, that day we had those pains, and our grandfather couldn't just get down in front of people like my little brother, he went off into the grass to be on his own. We had to keep up, the man who led us always kept telling us, we must catch up, but we asked him to wait for our grandfather.

So everyone waited for our grandfather to catch up. But he didn't. It was the middle of the day; insects were singing in our ears and we couldn't hear him moving through the grass. We couldn't see him because the grass was so high and he was so small. But he must have been somewhere there inside his loose trousers and his shirt that was torn and our grandmother couldn't sew because she had no cotton. We knew he couldn't have gone far because he was weak and slow. We all went to look for him, but in groups, so we too wouldn't be hidden from each other in that grass. It got into our eyes and noses; we called him softly but the noise of the insects must have filled the little space left for hearing in his ears. We looked and looked but we couldn't find him. We stayed in that long grass all night. In my sleep I found him curled round in a place he had tramped down for himself, like the places we'd seen where the buck hide their babies.

When I woke up he still wasn't anywhere. So we looked again, and by now there were paths we'd made by going through the grass many times, it would be easy for him to find us if we couldn't find him. All that day we just sat and waited. Everything is very quiet when the sun is on your head, inside your head, even if you lie, like the animals, under the trees. I lay on my back and saw those ugly birds with hooked beaks and plucked necks flying round and round above us. We had passed them often where they were feeding on the bones of dead animals, nothing was ever left there for us to eat. Round and round, high up and then lower down and then high again. I saw their necks poking to this side and that. Flying round and round. I saw our grandmother, who sat up all the time with my little brother on her lap, was seeing them, too.

In the afternoon the man who led us came to our grandmother and told her the other people must move on. He said, If their children don't eat soon they will die.

Our grandmother said nothing.

I'll bring you water before we go, he told her.

Our grandmother looked at us, me, my first-born brother, and my little brother on her lap. We watched the other people getting up to leave. I didn't believe the grass would be empty, all around us, where they had been. That we would be alone in this place, the Kruger Park, the police or the animals would find us. Tears came out of my eyes and nose on to my hands but our grandmother took no notice. She got up, with her feet apart the way she puts them when she is going to lift firewood, at home in our village, she

116

swung my little brother on to her back, tied him in her cloth – the top of her dress was torn and her big breasts were showing but there was nothing in them for him. She said, Come.

So we left the place with the long grass. Left behind. We went with the others and the man who led us. We started to go away, again.

There's a very big tent, bigger than a church or a school, tied down to the ground. I didn't understand that was what it would be, when we got there, away. I saw a thing like that the time our mother took us to the town because she heard our soldiers were there and she wanted to ask them if they knew where our father was. In that tent, people were praying and singing. This one is blue and white like that one but it's not for praying and singing, we live in it with other people who've come from our country. Sister from the clinic says we're 200 without counting the babies, and we have new babies, some were born on the way through the Kruger Park.

Inside, even when the sun is bright it's dark and there's a kind of whole village in there. Instead of houses each family has a little place closed off with sacks or cardboard from boxes – whatever we can find – to show the other families it's yours and they shouldn't come in even though there's no door and no windows and no thatch, so that if you're standing up and you're not a small child you can see into everybody's house. Some people have even made paint from ground rocks and drawn designs on the sacks.

Of course, there really is a roof – the tent is the roof, far, high up. It's like a sky. It's like a mountain and we're inside it; through the cracks paths of dust lead down, so thick you think you could climb them. The tent keeps off the rain overhead but the water comes in at the sides and in the little streets between our places – you can only move along them one person at a time – the small kids like my little brother play in the mud. You have to step over them. My little brother doesn't play. Our grandmother takes him to the clinic when the doctor comes on Mondays. Sister says there's something wrong with his head, she thinks it's because we didn't have enough food at home. Because of the war. Because our father wasn't there. And then because he was so hungry in the Kruger Park. He likes just to lie about on our grandmother all day, on her lap or against her somewhere and he looks at us and looks at us. He wants to ask something but you can see he can't. If I tickle him he may just smile. The clinic gives us special powder to make into porridge for him and perhaps one day he'll be all right.

When we arrived we were like him – my first-born brother and I. I can hardly remember. The people who lived in the village near the tent took us to the clinic, it's where you have to sign that you've come – away, through the Kruger Park. We sat on the grass and everything was muddled. One Sister was pretty with her hair straightened and beautiful high-heeled shoes and she brought us the special powder. She said we must mix it with water and drink it slowly. We tore the packets open with our teeth and licked it all up, it stuck round my mouth and I sucked it from my lips and fingers. Some other children who had walked with us vomited. But I only felt everything in my belly moving, the stuff going down and around like a snake, and hiccups hurt me. Another Sister called us to stand in line on the veranda of the clinic but we couldn't. We sat all over the place there, falling against each other: the Sisters helped each of us up by the arm and then stuck a needle in it. Other needles drew our blood into tiny bottles. This was against sickness, but I didn't understand, every time my eyes dropped closed I thought I was walking, the grass was long. I saw the elephants, I didn't know we were away.

But our grandmother was still strong, she could still stand up, she knows how to write and she signed for us. Our grandmother got us this place in the tent against one of the sides, it's the best kind of place there because although the rain comes in, we can lift the flap when the weather is good and then the sun shines on us, the smells in the tent go out. Our grandmother knows a woman here who showed her where there is good grass for sleeping mats, and our grandmother made some for us. Once every month the food truck comes to the clinic. Our grandmother takes along one of the cards she signed and when it has been punched we get a sack of mealie meal. There are wheelbarrows to take it back to the tent:

my first-born brother does this for her and then he and the other boys have races, steering the empty wheelbarrows back to the clinic. Sometimes he's lucky and a man who's bought beer in the village gives him money to deliver it – though that's not allowed, you're supposed to take that wheelbarrow straight back to the Sisters. He buys a cold drink and shares it with me if I catch him. On another day, every month, the church leaves a pile of old clothes in the clinic yard. Our grandmother has another card to get punched, and then we can choose something: I have two dresses, two pants and a jersey, so I can go to school.

The people in the village have let us join their school. I was surprised to find they speak our language; our grandmother told me, That's why they allow us to stay on their land. Long ago, in the time of our fathers, there was no fence that kills you, there was no Kruger Park between them and us, we were the same people under our own king, right from our village we left to this place we've come to.


Now that we've been in the tent so long – I have turned eleven and my little brother is nearly three although he is so small, only his head is big, he's not come right in it yet – some people have dug up the bare ground around the tent and planted beans and mealies and cabbage. The old men weave branches to put up fences round their gardens. No one is allowed to look for work in the towns but some of the women have found work in the village and can buy things. Our grandmother, because she's still strong, finds work where people are building houses – in this village the people build nice houses with bricks and cement, not mud like we used to have at our home. Our grandmother carries bricks for these people and fetches baskets of stones on her head. And so she has money to buy sugar and tea and milk and soap. The store gave her a calendar she has hung up on our flap of the tent. I am clever at school and she collected advertising paper people throw away outside the store and covered my school-books with it. She makes my first-born brother and me do our homework every afternoon before it gets dark because there is no room except to lie down, close

119

together, just as we did in the Kruger Park, in our place in the tent, and candles are expensive. Our grandmother hasn't been able to buy herself a pair of shoes for church yet, but she has bought black school shoes and polish to clean them with for my first-born brother and me. Every morning, when people are getting up in the tent, the babies are crying, people are pushing each other at the taps outside and some children are already pulling the crusts of porridge off the pots we ate from last night, my first-born brother and I clean our shoes. Our grandmother makes us sit on our mats with our legs straight out so she can look carefully at our shoes to make sure we have done it properly. No other children in the tent have real school shoes. When we three look at them it's as if we are in a real house again, with no war, no away.

Some white people came to take photographs of our people living in the tent – they said they were making a film, I've never seen what that is though I know about it. A white woman squeezed into our space and asked our grandmother questions which were told to us in our language by someone who understands the white woman's.

'How long have you been living like this?'

'She means here?' Our grandmother said. 'In this tent, two years and one month.'

'And what do you hope for the future?'

'Nothing. I'm here.'

'But for your children?'

'I want them to learn so that they can get good jobs and money.'

'Do you hope to go back to your own country?'

'I will not go back.'

'But when the war is over – your won't be allowed to stay here? Don't you want to go home?'

I didn't think our grandmother wanted to speak again. I didn't think she was going to answer the white woman. The white woman put her head on one side and smiled at us.

Our grandmother looked away from her and spoke. 'There is nothing. No home.'

Why does our grandmother say that? Why? I'll go back. I'll go back through that Kruger Park. After the war, if there are no bandits any more, our mother may be waiting for us. And maybe when we left our grandfather, he was only left behind, he found his way somehow, slowly, through the Kruger Park, and he'll be there. They'll be home, and I'll remember them.